Riding to Camille

Mary Buford Hitz

9/14/14

Riding to Camille

Mary Buford Hitz

Authorspress Publishing, LLC
Charlottesville, Virginia

F
Hit

Published by

AuthorsPress

Authorspress Publishing, LLC
Charlottesville, VA

Printed in the United States of America

Cover design by Claudia Miranda and Mayapriya Long
Text by Mayapriya Long, Bookwrights.com

ISBN: 978-1-940857-01-5

I dedicate this book to Fred, Eliza, Randy, Nathaniel and Willis, whose love keeps me cranking, and to the Virginia Center for the Creative Arts, a haven of mental and physical isolation for artists and writers.

DEBTS I OWE

To me, this book does not feel like historical fiction, but it *is* a novel whose structure and emotional heart are centered on Hurricane Camille, which devastated the Gulf Coast and Central Virginia in August of 1969.

Long before I realized that I wanted to embark on this novel, I was drawn to the intensity and peculiarity of Hurricane Camille's track through Nelson County, a part of Virginia that I know and love. The fact that twenty-nine inches of rain fell in five hours, for the most part in the dark, creates a cold fear deep in my being whenever I think about it.

I have roamed the files on Camille when they were in the Nelson County Library in Lovingston, Virginia; spent a research addict's hours pouring over torn and yellowed newspaper accounts of the worst and the best in people that the rescue efforts brought out; visited the Camille Center at Oakland, site of the Nelson County Historical Society; and attended lectures at the anniversary commemorations given by those whose lives were blown apart by the storm.

Over and above all of this miscellaneous information, there are three books that have informed my work with both scientific fact and with the human story.

The first, *Torn Land*, by Jerry H. Simpson, Jr. and his wife, Paige Shoaf Simpson, was published a year after the hurricane, in 1970. At the time, Jerry was associate editor of *The Daily Progress* newspaper in Charlottesville. The Simpsons lived in Waynesboro, just over the Blue Ridge Mountains, in the Shenandoah Valley. As one would expect, there is a horrifying immediacy and some confusion in this account, as the Simpsons were interviewing both victims and rescuers as the story was unfolding.

The second, *Category 5: The Story of Camille,* by Ernest Zebrowski and Judith A. Howard, was published in 2005. This account, unlike *Torn Land,* tells the stories of victims along the Gulf Coast as well as those in Nelson County.

The third is *Roar of the Heavens* by Stefan Bechtel, published in 2006. This was the most valuable to me, as Bechtel went to great lengths to understand, and then interpret for the lay reader, how Camille collected such destructive power before hitting the Gulf Coast, followed by the unusual convergence of conditions that caused it to come alive again over Nelson County.

These books make up my Camille bible. Although I don't quote from them, I use them throughout the novel. I owe their authors a debt of gratitude for their work; it made mine both easier and more interesting.

ONE

SAM CRAWFORD PAUSED ON HIS WALK up from the barn to the house on the hillside of Whiskey Ridge Farm, looking out over the broad, green expanse of the Rockfish Valley of Virginia. He was amazed at how the on-and-off rains of these last couple of weeks in mid-August of 1969 had greened up the landscape.

Though he had to to leave soon for the Charlottesville Albemarle Airport, he loaned himself the time to stand there and admire the gentle humps of the Blue Ridge Mountains, comfortably rounded and earth-anchored, much more a part of the earth than of the sky. The mountains, shimmering in the blue haze for which they were famous, had occasional shafts of late-afternoon sunlight cutting through the humidity, backlighting the marching stands of hardwoods along the ridge crests.

Sam was a stocky six-footer with curly sandy hair and the kind of good looks that come from a bodily impression of power. Farm work had strengthened his arms and legs, his shoulders and back, to the point where he found it far easier to do most jobs than to ask for someone else's help. So much did his jeans look a part of him that it seemed as if he must have put them on wet and let them dry along the contours of his skin. His light-cotton tee-shirt also mirrored the muscle underneath. Who could say whether its buckwheat color was chosen to go with his hazel eyes, or whether this was just an accident. Sam had an air of competence about him, as if he had yet to see a problem that would stump him.

Reluctantly turning from the view of the mountains, Sam noticed his wife standing on the porch, watching him as he approached. "Odd weather, Elsie," he said. She nodded her head, concurring silently. "These thunderstorms must be what's making the plane late," he said.

"Did you leave money so I can stock up on groceries for next week's riding trip?" asked Elsie in her pointed way, knowing that she would have to remind him several times more before he would come up with it in a day or so. Her question left Sam silent, irritated as usual by her change of subject, and he brushed past her abruptly through the door on the way to get his keys. She heard the screen door slam shut at the back of the house as he hurried off.

Sam was on his way to meet their arriving guest, Lisl Stern, a young Swiss woman who had first come two years ago to help with the horseback riding tours that Sam and Elsie led. At first the young summer intern had helped only with farm chores: picking and weeding the vegetable garden and helping Elsie prepare and package the food that went out on the rides, for Lisl had no experience with horses.

Sam had his own methods of dealing with the farm's horses. He disliked trying to teach people who came with their own ideas; it was so much simpler if they just did what he said and followed his horse routines.

But as that first summer wore on, Sam was surprised and pleased to discover that Lisl had, in fact, a natural affinity for the large, beautiful, dangerous, instinct-driven animal that is the horse. Her temperament contained the perfect combination of fearlessness and caution for dealing with horses. She had her way with them not through coercion, but through the gentle confidence with which she treated them. Sam couldn't understand where that confidence came from—it seemed to have always been there. Yet Lisl might have lived her entire life without ever encountering a horse.

Lisl gravitated toward work at the barn that summer, and she soon was helping Sam with the horses—and learning to ride. Instructions that Sam felt he had to tell their guests the Biblical seventy-times-seven, such as to put a hand on a horse's rump before walking behind it, Lisl knew instinctively and never had to be told.

He taught her to tie a slip knot—useful with horses because it slips loose with one quick jerk—in one brief session, her earlobe-length straight blond hair falling forward over her face as she leaned towards him, her arresting blue eyes intent on his demonstration. She was a slip of a young woman, of medium height but seemingly taller, her thin, boyish figure so erect and purposeful.

Despite her slight frame, Lisl was deceptively strong, able to lift a bale of hay or a sack of feed that weighed half as much as she did. Sam had had to rethink his ideas of what women could accomplish; the first time Lisl had seen him reattaching a horse's thrown shoe, she had wanted to know how it was done.

He showed her, certain that she wouldn't be able to steady the horse's heavy leg, or gauge correctly the place in a horse's hoof where nerve cells begin and nails cannot be driven. He had been wrong on both counts, and he also noticed that horses were less restive under Lisl's hand as she spoke to them in her conversational voice about what was happening as she worked with them.

By the second summer she regularly was going out with the guest riders. She quickly learned the trails so that she could lead the groups if sick livestock or a farm emergency kept Sam homebound. When Elsie fell behind in her food preparations for a trip, or felt overwhelmed with bed changes, Lisl noticed, and, without being asked, would lend another pair of hands.

Soon Sam and Elsie came to trust her thoroughly. She fit

into their life as if she were the child they never had, but without any of the natural friction that often arises when daughters work for parents. By the end of the second summer, they had begun to talk to Lisl about the possibility of her getting a green card for lawful permanent residence, with an eye toward one day moving to Virginia.

As Sam drove his old pickup truck around the Charlottesville bypass, a radio announcer's voice caught his attention. Dr. Robert Simpson of the National Hurricane Center announced that the tropical storm headed from the Cayman Islands toward Cuba had become a Category 3 hurricane, named Camille. No wonder we've been having so much rain, Sam thought, heading north on U.S. 29 toward the airport.

Sam knew that Lisl's visit would be a watershed. Since she was so clearly gifted with animals and had taken so quickly to the routines of farming, Sam and Elsie found it hard to believe that, for this last year in Switzerland, Lisl had worked as a clerk for an American law firm.

She had not gone to university, but her International Baccalaureate diploma had given her a solid grounding in English and basic business skills; in addition, the law firm had insisted that she take an intensive English language course. After six weeks of the course, she could have passed for an American.

The life Lisl was leading in Switzerland now took her farther and farther away from the world of her childhood sweetheart, Hans Werther, who worked as a blacksmith. He was joining her on this trip to Virginia to see firsthand the place that now exerted such a strong pull on his girlfriend. Sam suspected that Lisl wanted to see if Hans was transferable—whether or not, with his very limited English and his suspicion of change, he could be talked into moving to Virginia with her. Of course, Hans' skills would make him very useful on the farm, if he chose to be.

When Sam got to the airport, he discovered that their international flight had arrived in New York on time. However,

violent thunderstorms in the mid-Atlantic region had tempo-
rarily grounded their Piedmont Airlines turbo prop, which
was to bring the visitors on the last leg of their trip from
Kennedy Airport to Charlottesville. While waiting, Sam had
plenty of time to speculate about their arrival, which he was
both looking forward to and dreading.

How had Lisl burrowed so quickly into their lives, easing
the sterile truce that had grown up between Elsie and him?
Would Hans, whom they had never met but had heard so
much about, accept them, too, or would they be the enemy?

A defeated airport air-conditioner pushed out more noise
than cool air as Sam's mind wandered back over the last
twenty years, wondering at the serendipity that had brought
him to this place in life. It wasn't that things felt pre-ordained,
exactly, but rather that situations and events had arisen and
then evolved without his having made any seemingly con-
scious choices.

He remembered the first time he had laid eyes on Elsie.
He had been a senior at Virginia Tech, about to graduate
with a degree in Animal Husbandry, with a part-time job
mucking stalls at a nearby stable each morning before classes
and on weekends.

One of the horses at the barn was a coal-black, stur-
dy-boned quarter horse gelding with an all-white face, which
gave him a questioning look. Most horses would stir about
uneasily if Sam came into a stall to refill a water bucket or
bring a wedge of hay, forcing Sam to maneuver around them
within the confines of their stalls.

But Jinks, short for Hijinks, would look up as Sam entered, and, without moving, would stop chewing altogether
and watch Sam with a Buddha-like gaze. After Sam had
finished whatever mission had brought him to Jinks's stall,
the horse's eyes would follow him down the wide aisle of the
stable until Sam was out of sight.

Jinks seemed quiet to the point of being stolid. It was
several months before Sam realized that he had seen all the

other horses at one point or another being ridden by someone, but never Jinks. He asked the barn manager about this and learned that the horse belonged to an older lady who had bought him to save him from being sold for horsemeat at a county livestock auction because she heard and saw that Jinks had a singular peculiarity.

Although Jinks was a quiet, well-mannered riding horse and a good jumper, he would instantly buck off anyone who came down in the saddle so as to touch off a sore spot on his back. It didn't happen often, but when it did, Jinks would explode with the kind of raw power that sent big men arcing over his head. After he had dismissed his rider, Jinks would stand still, surveying the scene and acting unrepentant, as if no explanation were needed. At various times, veterinarians declared that Jinx's back was cured, but then Jinks would throw another rider, which is how the horse ended up at the livestock auction.

At the auctions, it was the job of Lucille Quigby to examine the livestock sales, looking for evidence of animal abuse on behalf of the local S.P.C.A. She had felt selected by Jinks's unblinking gaze and bought him for a pittance after learning why he was there. She never tried to ride him, but she loved to come to the stable, feed him carrots, walk him on a lead line to where the grass was greenest for grazing, and occasionally work him on a lunge line in the paddock.

Elsie Lyons, who had graduated from Virginia Tech four years before, worked as the bookkeeper at the stables and was always looking for horses to ride, since she couldn't afford to own one herself. Seeing that Jinks was never ridden, she approached his owner and asked if she could ride him.

Lucille explained to her about Jinks and his back, saying that as much as she would love to see him ridden, she didn't want to have anyone else get hurt. But Elsie pressed Lucille to let her ride him, and, against her better judgment, Lucille gave in. Expecting to feel both guilty and responsible when

Elsie was thrown off, Lucille instead watched an unusual bond form between horse and rider.

Elsie was short, carrying no extra weight on her small bones. Her gray eyes were hard to read, with mouse-brown hair and bangs that framed an unremarkable face. What was remarkable about her was the economy of movement expressed in her frame, even on a horse.

Sam had been out in the ring one weekend afternoon, raking the surface to redistribute the dirt that piled up in front of the jumps, when a noise from the woods on the hillside above the ring caused him to look up. His eyes rose just in time to see Elsie trot Jinks out of the woods and then, shunning the gate, jump downhill over a sizeable chicken coop into the pasture.

The grade at the jump was steep enough to make Elsie lean back in the saddle, holding the reins higher than usual and bracing her feet in the stirrups against the landing. As the big horse resumed his trot down the hill, Elsie's body effortlessly came forward in the saddle and picked back up the rhythm of the trot.

Many riders appear as mere passengers on a horse, an inert weight that the horse must carry around. But as Elsie and Jinks descended gradually across the pasture, Elsie's body was synchronized with Jinks, her legs feeling the rhythm of his gait through the saddle, her hands with the reins in them moving along his neck to check his pace and then give him his head again, her hips a center of gravity matching the downhill grade and keeping her torso poised upright, leaning neither backwards nor forwards.

Sam, who had grown up riding, had a shiver of recognition, as he watched a difficult maneuver instinctively well-performed, that he was watching a talented horsewoman.

As she approached she slowed her horse to a walk. Sam stopped his work, and leaning his rake on the ring's fencing, hailed her and introduced himself. They went out for a beer that evening, and although when he saw her off the horse he noted that she wasn't beautiful, he was intrigued by her sparse, effective movements. They dated the rest of his senior year.

He had been nonplussed by the detachment which she showed toward him. Sam had had a series of girlfriends at Tech and had gotten used to being in control of how things went; he had never had to work hard for his conquests. Four years older than he, Elsie seemed on the one hand to take his attentions for granted, and on the other to be reconciled to his disappearance in advance.

And that might have happened if his father had not died unexpectedly two months before graduation, leaving him, as an only child, to realize that if he and his mother didn't want to sell their Nelson County farm where he had grown up, he needed to move back home and take up where his father had left off. In the confusion of the weeks immediately following his father's death, when Elsie had come home with him on weekends to help his mother, he became aware of how seamlessly she fit into the routine.

His father had raised Hereford cattle, kept a few horses, and taken hay from the pastures. He had grown corn on the farm's only bottomland, where Luther's Creek formed the valley boundary of their property, and had horse-logged the slopes of Long Arm Mountain with dangerous and beautiful skill.

Sam's mother raised vegetables and fruits in the garden between the barn and the house, fed her pigs with table scraps, and raised chickens in the wired henhouse at the other end of the barn from the pigsty. The Crawfords were land poor, but they owned seven hundred acres of some of the most beautiful and varied land in the state, half in the valley and half on the mountain. It had gotten them by for three generations, not without work that tested the limits of human endurance, Sam thought, but also without ever going hungry.

On the weekends Elsie took over the horse operations. She distributed hay, gave the horses their feed and immunizations, and worked with the young colts and fillies, allowing Sam to concentrate on the cows and spring planting.

Sam's mother seemed not to question the young woman's odd combination of energy and wordlessness. Dazed by her own loss, Mrs. Crawford was half-glad that Elsie moved about silently, doing what needed doing, as unobtrusive as a servant in an eighteenth-century Dutch painting. The week before his graduation, Sam had taken the course of least resistance and asked Elsie to marry him, and had not been surprised when she agreed.

Elsie was spare with words, kept her thoughts to herself, and appeared to have no temper at all. They were opposites; in fact, the only trait they shared was an affinity for work, which was always their strongest bond. He knew that he was really asking her to marry the farm, and that this was all right with her. She understood animals better than humans, he had come to realize.

Their sex, furtive and fast on the single bed in Sam's room when his mother left the farm to drive to Nellysford to pick up the mail, seemed more to do with the animal kingdom than the human one. It was a physically satisfying release, but when it was over he was left with the feeling that he was simply a vehicle for pleasure; sought more for the tidal pull of his mouth on her breast, or the feel of his hand on her inner thigh, than for any sense that two souls, not just two bodies, were joined.

After they were married they were subsumed by the work of the farm. His mother continued to live with them, exchanging her room with theirs: Elsie and Sam took over the bigger bedroom with the old, four-poster bed with windows facing the valley, and his mother moved into Sam's old room, looking out on the holly and the big magnolia in the backyard and the slope rising behind the house.

What they had in abundance was land and beauty all around them, plus a network of colonial-era dirt roads, logging trails, fire roads, and riding trails that made possible the business they had developed: leading horseback riding trips of one to three days.

Over a decade they had done less and less farming, selling the cattle and growing only what they and their horses needed to eat. Sam spent long hours acquiring farmers' permission to ride over their lands, and he had wrestled from U.S. Forest Service officials the right to use the fire and logging roads on the mountain land in the George Washington National Forest across the valley from the farm.

Under Sam's father, draft horses did the farm work and the logging. But once the Crawfords made the decision to lead pleasure rides, they built up the herd. They culled over time in order to get horses with enough stamina for long rides; enough bone strength and size to deal well with steep slopes, bad footing and big customers; and temperaments gentle enough for indifferent riders. Their first few years, before they had been able to build up a core of trained riding horses, had been lean indeed.

Sam's mother died a few years after his father, leaving them not only with one less set of hands for the work to be done, but also without the buffer that had kept Sam and Elsie from having to confront their own incompatibility. Meanwhile, Elsie suffered an atrophic pregnancy that was discovered late; because they lived so far from medical help, it almost caused her to bleed to death.

Since that time she had been unable to conceive, and the time and money it would have taken to seek medical help from a fertility specialist was spent instead, ironically, on their equine breeding and training program, and on vet bills.

They settled into a state of more or less permanent physical exhaustion, unpaid bills, and mutual recognition that they needed each other; it led to a kind of psychic truce in their marriage. Lisl's presence helped in some ways: she dealt with the rider guests, showing a comfort and confidence with strangers. Sam was the horse outfitter, matching people with the right horses to get a group prepared, and Elsie was the provisioner, with her working attention to detail. Sam's chief frustration came when guests didn't catch on quickly to instructions. Sometimes he didn't go on the rides, but stayed behind to work, training horses.

They took rides out only in the spring, early summer and fall, leaving the winter months for logging and farm upkeep. Usually they didn't take any riders out in August when the heat was at its worst, but they made an exception this year: Lisl and Hans could come for only three weeks, starting in mid-August. Sam and Elsie booked a three-day ride, due to start August 17, two days after Lisl and Hans arrived.

The ride needed Sam, Elsie and Lisl to ensure a smooth trip; one of the guest riders was writing a story for the magazine *Chronicle of the Horse*. In addition, Sam's cousin Tad Crawford, who spoke pigeon German learned from his service in the U.S. Army at Dusseldorf, was coming to stay on the farm with Hans while the riders were away. Hans would shoe the horses not being used on the ride, while Tad would drive the tractor to spread manure in the pastures, a job Sam never seemed to have time for because there was always something more pressing to be done.

At the airport, Sam's reverie ended when he heard a gravelly, disembodied voice announced the arrival of the Piedmont flight from New York. He rose from a row of seats and walked toward the gate to meet his exhausted travelers.

Lisl and Hans had been up before dawn: they took a train to Geneva, flew on an uneventful trip from Geneva to New York, and then waited four hours for their flight south. To their bodies, it was two o'clock in the morning Swiss time when the 8 p.m. flight arrived from New York; the turbo-prop had bounced around in the humid atmosphere, making stomach-churning moves sideways as it found its way down onto the runway at Charlottesville.

After twenty-two hours traveling, Lisl wanted only to sleep. Hans had slept on the plane, but such rest always eluded her. As the two emerged from the plane, a wall of moist, warm air hit them, better than the fetid air of the plane, Lisl thought. Fierce in its promise of the heat to come tomorrow, an enormous flaming-red sun banked behind the mountains on the other side of the runway from the boxy brick airport.

As they approached the terminal, Lisl saw Sam waving to attract their attention, a wide smile on his face. Hans, who had been walking a few paces behind her, caught up and put his arm over her shoulder as if to remind her of his presence.

"Hey, girl," said Sam, reaching her first and giving her a bear hug, "so glad you're back." Before Lisl could introduce Hans, Sam turned to him, grabbed his hand, and welcomed him to Virginia.

"Glad to meet you," said Hans, using one of his few well-rehearsed phrases.

"Any friend of Lisl's is doubly welcome," said Sam, shepherding them over to the baggage carousel.

TWO

Elsie knelt on top of the mattress of the rickety bed in the old smokehouse, tucking in the sheets on the wall side. The wedding ring quilted bedspread, folded at the foot of the bed, had lost most of its color and batting to repeated washings over the years, but it was all Lisl and Hans would need for cover in this weather, and besides, it added a little style to this otherwise bare room.

Lisl and Sam would stay in these sparse quarters because they needed to save the bedrooms in the house for the riding guests. The guests would arrive mid-afternoon the day before the ride and be matched with horses and saddles, familiarizing themselves with the camping equipment that they would use on the trip.

Since the trip's first night was always spent at the house, it fell to Elsie to prepare the rooms and cook a welcoming dinner, while at the same time seeing to the checklist of supplies needed for the trip.

Once, when she had stayed home to mind the farm, she had accidently left out toilet paper. When the ride came in three days later and Elsie went out to hold horses and help everyone unload their packs, Sam had announced in a loud voice, "For God's sake woman, you forgot the toilet paper— how could you? Forgetting the bum wad is grounds for divorce, right, folks?" As in so many other times in her life, Elsie said nothing, but instead just turned away to tie up a packhorse.

Not that Sam would even think to mention or thank her for the 45 items on the checklist that *had* made it into the packs of provisions, even if she had forgotten the T.P. After all, Elsie always sent them off with double the number of paper napkins usually needed, so it wasn't as if they'd had a crisis, was it? It was just a good chance for Sam to embarrass her publicly.

Actually, it was the guests who looked embarrassed by Sam's comment; they didn't answer back. Most of the women and a few of the men shot Elsie sympathetic glances.

She sighed, backed off the bed on her knees, stood up, and thought to herself that, even if Lisl and Hans' quarters weren't fancy, they were clean, and had a lovely view of the apple and peach trees to one side of the house. After all, their quarters were better than the tool shed where she and Sam would unroll their own sleeping bags and air mattresses the night when the guests were in the house.

As she left, she straightened the frayed hook rug with her foot and assured a cross draft by opening a window and shutting just the screen door opposite it. Traversing the few yards between the shed and the kitchen backdoor, she passed the dogs.

Willa, a yellow lab, and Turtle, a mutt, made up of a cross between something that was substantial with something else that was just the opposite, were laid out in the shade of the sycamore tree, hard by the house.

"Hey, wigglies," she called out to them, using their communal nickname because they would try to wiggle themselves onto her lap if they found her seated. Noting a woman on a mission, they didn't budge, but flopped their tails a couple of times on the ground to signal their greeting.

She entered the screened porch that stretched along the back of the house where they lived this time of year, and crossed through it to the cramped, narrow kitchen. It had the air of being planned by a man, or at least by someone who didn't cook. The only counter space was to either side of the sink on one side of the room; the other side had an old gas stove at one end and glass-fronted cabinets floor-to-ceiling down the rest of the wall. Worn linoleum curled upward at the edges of the floor. They had planned to enclose the screen porch eventually and make that the kitchen, but hope of that had vanished with the drought and crop losses and hadn't been mentioned since.

It was ironic that they actually had big square rooms: the front parlor with its stiff Victorian sofas and worn oriental rugs, and the dining room with its heavy dark-mahogany claw-footed table. They almost never used them. The dining room became their workroom in the winter, but this time of year Sam worked on his accounts or watched sports on television on the screened porch when he was indoors.

As she stood at the sink peeling carrots, she thought about what was available in the garden to serve for supper the day after tomorrow, when the riding guests would arrive. The cabbage was a bit wormy, but she could cut around the bad spots, and if she missed a few, she figured that a little extra protein wouldn't hurt anybody.

Sautéed with onions and garlic, the cabbage would go well with a pork roast. Plus the beets were still doing well. They always had plenty of potatoes, and the tomatoes, as usual, were falling off the vine, so she would use them both, as a salad, with lots of chopped herbs.

She was beginning to make herself hungry, so she ate a spoonful of the gazpacho she had made for tonight's dinner— that is, if Sam ever arrived home with Lisl and Hans. He had called to say their plane was late, but he hadn't known when it might arrive, so everything was on hold.

Late suited her, as it would give her time to make and freeze the scrambled egg and Canadian bacon sandwiches that had proven so popular on the trail. They had a freezer in the basement that they kept at a low enough temperature to freeze food so solidly that it took a day to defrost, which it did nicely in the food hampers on the backs of the packhorses.

As she worked, Elsie savored the silence around her. She loved having the place to herself, just her and the animals, wild and domesticated. At night, when she was alone on the farm, she liked to turn off all the lights and sit, listening, on the screened porch.

If a front was coming through, she could hear the subdued roar of the wind at the top of the ridge above the house, sounding like a freight train heard from afar. If it was a quiet night, she could hear the actual freight trains bound for the Shenandoah Valley. She could hear them laboring as they pulled up the steep grade on Afton Mountain that would take them to the Crozet tunnel under the mountain, and on into the valley. As soon as they entered the tunnel, their noise abruptly ceased.

If she stayed there long enough, she could hear mice and chipmunks moving in the walls of the old house, and the snuffling noise that deer make as they breathe out. She could imagine them extending their necks to get at the lowest-hanging apples in the old orchard. If she spoke to the deer in a low voice, they stopped what they were doing and looked toward the porch without moving, but if she rose out of the chair, they bounded off, each of them scattering in a different direction.

She seldom rose, as she figured the deer were entitled to the first fruits, at least of the August apples. Now, in another month when the Pippins came in, that was another matter: she would fight for every last one of those. They weren't lookers, Pippins, but their sassy, fight-back taste and texture made them a baker's prize apple.

Looking up, she caught the headlights of their truck, dipping and rising through the potholes in the driveway, coming toward the house as Sam rounded the curve by the barn. Elsie dried her hands on her apron, untied it and threw it on the back of a chair, checked in the little wall mirror to see that she didn't look any worse than usual, and went out to welcome Lisl and Hans.

Late the next morning, skim-milk sunlight pierced the haze as steam from the night's thunderstorm rose from the old brick pavement where the truck was parked. As Sam came by the shed on his way to the house, he could hear the low murmur of Lisl and Hans, talking in German. As he headed for the screened porch, he heard them scuffling, followed by laughter and a quick succession of thudding noises that sounded like the start of a pillow fight.

He felt a surge of annoyance at—he wasn't sure what— how young they were? How carefree? How foreign to him the thought of sleeping late? How long it had been since even the thought of a pillow fight, much less a vacation, had so much as crossed his mind?

In the kitchen, Elsie heard the screen door slap shut as Sam came in and kicked off his rubber work boots on a strip of old carpeting by the door. The drought of the last few summers had been replaced by the uncharacteristically wet weather of this summer, and mud manufactured in the last couple of weeks had made an under-layer of red clay soil on his boots, with bits of straw sticking out of it.

He picked up a boot in each hand and, holding the screen door open with his foot, hit each against the side of the house until the extra sole of mud fell away behind the box bushes that crowded close to the door. There used to be a metal dachshund whose long back was covered with bristles so that you could wipe your boots on it before coming onto the porch. But one leg had given way, it had pitched ignominiously onto its nose, and weeds had all but buried it.

"That you, Sam?" called Elsie, coming from the kitchen with a lunch tray of sandwiches and a pitcher of iced tea.

"Yup," he replied, "and I don't think Lisl and Hans will be far behind. I heard them as I came by the shed."

Last evening Elsie's good food had revived the young

couple, and the four of them had stayed up talking, knowing that the travelers could sleep in the next morning. That is, Sam and Lisl had talked. Hans was limited to a few English phrases, although Sam suspected that he understood what was said fairly well but was too unsure of himself to venture to speak. Elsie, never very talkative, had mostly listened.

Sam lit into his BLT sandwich. The heat had taken away Elsie's appetite, so she didn't object when he swooped up half of her sandwich after finishing his, as the ice tea in the pitcher quickly disappeared.

"Can't use Prudence on the ride," Sam reported. "She's off on her left front foot. I didn't see any obvious problem, and she turns all right, so it's not her shoulder. Hope to hell it isn't an abscess, but I took her shoe off just in case. DAMN. If it is an abscess we won't be here to soak it."

They had been sure they would use Pru on the ride; she was quiet and would have been the perfect mount for Stanley Gibson, the *Chronicle* writer's husband, who had ridden only once before, in childhood. Elsie, knowing that they couldn't afford to call the vet except in extreme cases, didn't reply. Sam, as if reading her mind, said "What a pity Hans isn't a vet."

Lisl and Hans, looking happy, well rested and slightly sheepish, came across the lawn toward the porch.

"Good morning, or rather good afternoon," teased Sam.

Elsie jumped up from the table as they came through the door. "I've saved some waffle batter for you; how about waffles and some scrambled eggs?"

"Oh, how wonderful," said Lisl, heading to the kitchen to lend a hand and remembering the half-cup of melted butter that went into Elsie's stone-ground graham flour waffle recipe.

Sam motioned Hans to a chair and asked him how he had slept.

"Thank you," responded Hans, obviously at a loss as he tried to interpret Sam's Piedmont Virginia accent. Sam pantomimed sleep, laying his head on his hands and snoring.

"Oh!" smiled Hans, understanding. "It was well." An awkward pause followed this communication until Hans ventured, "It is most hot here Switzerland," falling back on the time-honored subject of the weather to rescue the conversation. And Sam, eager to keep this line going, launched into an involved description of how Virginia's infamous humidity made even modestly hot temperatures seem unbearable.

Elsie and Lisl reappeared carrying breakfast as advertised, with the extra touch of bacon crumbled over the eggs. "Sam," said Elsie, "don't go on so about the heat. It's bad enough without talking about it." Hans, grateful not to have to talk anymore, dug into his breakfast.

Lisl, Elsie and Sam fell into a discussion about the ride, with Sam giving a thumbnail sketch of the guest riders who were due to arrive tomorrow afternoon. For the past several years he had tried to interest magazines and newspapers in sending a journalist who could take the trip and then write about it, but the answer was always that it required too much time.

Lisl could hear the excitement in his voice as he described the person whom the *Chronicle of the Horse* was sending. "Her name is Lenore Gibson and she's an assistant editor. She's been on horseback riding tours in France and Hungary and was surprised to find a Virginia ride. She's very interested in horses—wants to make them a big part of the story—and she's going to do her own photography."

"She asked if it would be possible to bring her husband along. He isn't a rider, although he rode a couple of times as a child; he must be in good shape because he used to run marathons. I said sure, since in the mountains we'll mostly be walking anyway. Told her I'd make sure he was on the safest horse of the lot."

"That would have been Prudence," said Elsie, "but she's gone and come up lame."

"What about Packer?" responded Lisl. Packer was a

four-year-old Lisl had broken to the saddle and trained the summer before. He got his name because he was unusually quiet-tempered and docile, even as a colt, and soon was packing around anyone they put on him, even children who had never ridden before.

In the springtime, Elsie gave a series of lessons at Whiskey Ridge Farm, and Packer went out-of-character only once during the three months she had ridden him every day. One morning she had decided to try using a pair of blunt spurs to force him to pay attention to her leg commands.

The first time she gently applied pressure on his flank with her heel, he shot into a fit of bucking, depositing her in a mud puddle at the corner of the ring. She got up slowly, took off the spurs, showed them to Packer as she put them aside, and got back on. The rest of their ring work proceeded as if the bucking had never happened. Packer also was smaller than most of the other horses, making it easy for a beginner to mount and dismount.

"Packer it will have to be," said Sam. "Make sure you give him a good workout this afternoon so he'll be reminded of his manners."

"Which horse are you going to put Lenore on?" queried Elsie, pretty sure she already knew. Sam hesitated, wanting to ride Challenger himself, but knowing that Lenore would have much more fun on the ride if she rode him. He admired the horse's high head carriage and the way he felt he looked on Challenger—properly in charge, commanding, even—and hated to give that up.

He also liked the horse's energy and stamina, and the way in which, with little urging, Challenger would walk faster when he was leading a group. This meant that Sam, if he found himself in front, didn't have to respond to all of the tiresome questions guests were continually asking. "Guess I'll have to give her Challenger," he said, resigned to the choice." "Then we know she'll write a good article."

"Who are the other riders?" asked Lisl. Elsie, who handled most of the correspondence with guests, filled her in.

"There's a couple coming from Washington, Meg and Will Lapsley, they're in their late fifties. They shouldn't be a problem, as they've ridden all their lives. And a young woman in the Foreign Service stationed in England named Sarah Feldcamp who rides on weekends. She's home for a couple of weeks, one week for consultations and one for vacation. Her mother had seen our ad in *The Washington Post*, that's how she knew about our rides."

Sam interjected, "It's a small group, which is great, because we'll have the time to tailor what we do for what would make for a good article in *The Chronicle*."

THREE

Lɪsʟ sᴀᴛ ᴏɴ ᴀ sᴛᴏᴏʟ ɪɴ ᴛʜᴇ ᴀɪsʟᴇ of the barn, the top of her torso leaning against the warm mass of Prudence's shoulder, her hand on the horse's leg in order to keep the abscessed foot soaking in the bucket of Epsom salts and warm water in front of them. Braless in the wet heat, she shook the top of her sleeveless cotton shirt with her free hand to push a feeble breeze towards her face.

Whenever she took her hand away or even let up on the pressure slightly, Pru, with stolid deliberation, would remove her foot, clanking the side of the aluminum bucket and sloshing water out of it. Whenever Lisl felt the horse's leg tensing, she would croon reassurance, "Hold tight old girl, this is doing you good. Just forget about your foot, and think about the carrots in my pocket instead."

As if on queue, Pru turned her massive head and butted Lisl in the general vicinity of her pocket, knocking her off the stool. Simultaneously she removed her foot from the bucket. Lisl picked herself up, laughing, resumed her position, and returned Pru's foot to the bucket.

Pru's was the classic build of a draft horse: compact, big-boned, with powerful shoulders that rose to a bulge of muscle below her withers, large rounded feet, and a hind end that, in tandem with her shoulders, gave her the engine needed to carry a heavy man up a mountain or pull a hundred-year-old tree out of the forest. Because of these near-perfect characteristics of the breed, she had been kept and bred many times. The history of her numerous foals showed in the sag of her belly.

As she again leaned against the horse, Lisl thought about all that they had accomplished yesterday, working through the long summer evening until daylight faded. In the morning, she and Elsie had cleaned upstairs and remade the beds in the master bedroom and in Sam's mother's old room for the two pairs of married guests.

They would put the single young woman in an alcove off the living room, separated from the rest of the room by a batik curtain. It had a cot in it piled high with old magazines, broken harness, a set of electric hair curlers, and indentations where the dogs had slept. They stashed what they could under the cot and made the space functional if not attractive.

Meanwhile Hans was double-checking the shoes of the horses to be used on the ride, while Sam cleaned off the tack for the five guest riders, setting the saddle, saddle blanket, bridle, and saddlebags for each horse on highboys outside the tack room. In the afternoon, Sam and Hans had gone down to the creek bottom to mend a weak point that would soon be a break in the fence, and to bush hog the wild grapevines threatening to take over the pasture.

Elsie stayed close to the phone in case there were last-minute changes of plan, while Lisl worked with a newly broke three-year-old colt, a chestnut with a striking white blaze on his face and white stockings on his two hind legs. He had balked when first brought in for training, loathe to leave his carefree existence in the pasture for one of work and discipline. After initial reluctance he had given in and now seemed to Lisl to look forward to being ridden.

She had worked in the makeshift ring on getting him to pay attention to the aides she gave him: pressure with her inside leg to steady him at a trot and to push him deep into the corners of the ring, pressure from both legs to keep the young horse moving forward at a consistent pace, alerts through the reins that he must tuck his head in, gather himself better and use his hind end instead of leaning heavily on the bit. She loved the patience and repetition required of that kind of riding. Nothing could be taken for granted because it was all new territory to the young horse.

Yesterday, after about twenty-five minutes of hard work, the colt suddenly stopped dead in his tracks and looked back at her with a quizzical expression as if to say, "My head hurts. Let's stop." She had laughed out loud at how put-upon he obviously felt. Although she couldn't let him decide when to stop, she realized she had been pushing him too hard; she made him walk forward a few paces and then pulled up, patted him for a good effort, and called it a day.

After supper they unzipped and aired the sleeping bags to be used on the trip, checking to see that each person's canvas supply bag had no mold on it or mice roosting in it. The most amazing things occasionally showed up—a dog's collar, a condom, pictures of nudes, joints, a rosary, packets of pills—all of which proved that guests paid only so much attention to the plea that went out in the early paperwork that they leave behind at home everything but the essentials. "Essential" was clearly open for interpretation.

They were all exhausted when the last bit of daylight was squeezed against the horizon to the west and finally dimmed completely; bedtime had come early. As Lisl lay next to Hans with her head on his extended arm and her arm stretched across his broad chest, she had sensed that his quietness was not just from fatigue, but that he was ill at ease. When she asked him what was wrong, he kissed her inquiring eyes, gently took her arm off his chest, and rolled the other way, saying without words that it was too hot to snuggle.

I know him, she thought, as well as I know myself. Let him be. He'll work it out, whatever "it" was. Instead of prodding him, she massaged his back with the palm of her free hand for a few seconds before the work of the day took its toll and she fell asleep.

The next morning Hans caught a ride into Waynesboro with Elsie, who was going to market to buy the perishables for the trip. He had wanted to go to mass at the Catholic Church, it being Sunday. This surprised Lisl, as he only went to church on holidays at home. Hans and Elsie drove off at mid-morning, promising to be home with cold cuts for a late lunch before the guests were due to arrive.

Early that morning, before the heat built up, Sam had climbed up Whiskey Ridge Mountain to check the outflow of the larger of the mountain springs that had seldom failed the farm. After finding it running well, he allowed himself the luxury of a quick visit to the most beautiful spot on the land that he owned. Climbing further to the rock outcropping at the top of the ridge, he scrambled to the edge and sat, dangling his legs over air.

Across the valley to the southwest was Humpback Mountain, high for these parts at more than three thousand feet. It was dominant in his view, its broad side reaching out to join Elk Mountain to the north. Humpback's southern arm turned and curled east, sending folds of successively smaller hillsides jutting out a third of the way across the valley toward where Sam sat, like a belt at the valley's mid-section.

These folds blocked his view of the larger, more imposing mountains of Three Ridges and the Priest, around the corner at the end of the Rockfish Valley. The southern end of Sam's view was formed by the Ragged Mountains, a disorderly procession of hills marching out from Charlottesville in Albemarle County toward Lovingston, the seat of Nelson County to the southwest.

To the north Afton Mountain closed in the third side of the valley, its two small promontories and the saddle between them reminiscent of a young woman with a bigger ribcage than bosoms. The southwestern slope of Afton Mountain petered out at Rockfish Gap before rising again to join long, flat-topped Elk Mountain.

The Gap, giving access to the much bigger Shenandoah Valley, had been a shortcut to the west for the Monacan Indians long before Claudius Crozet tunneled under it for the railroad, and before Stonewall Jackson and his cavalry used its mountain trails to disappear back into the hills after lightening raids on unsuspecting Federal troops in the Shenandoah Valley during the Civil War.

Now, in 1969, the Gap was the only scar on a landscape of incredible pastoral beauty. An east-west interstate highway was under construction, twin ribbons of asphalt rising to the Gap along the northeastern slopes of Afton Mountain, tangling at Rockfish Gap with the state road it was superseding, the northern end of the Skyline Drive, the beginning of the Blue Ridge Parkway, the Appalachian Trail, and a Howard Johnson's motel and restaurant.

The scarring was not so much from the interstate itself as from the gouges made into the side of the mountain to make way for the gradual ascent the interstate had to maintain. Shale had eventually given way to dynamite, but successive cuts in the unstable sections of the mountain left raw walls of gray rock and red earth to show where the interstate was eating its way across the landscape.

Behind Sam the Rockfish Valley was open-ended, blending into the Piedmont Valley, a rolling forested land of hardwoods broken up by open pastures and farms all the way east to Charlottesville.

Looking at his watch, Sam jumped up, picked his way off the rock and scrambled down the trail, digging his heels into the stony earth to check his speed as he loped downward. He had work to do in the office before keeping his promise to help Lisl with stable chores.

Lisl was just wondering how much longer to soak the hoof when the sunlight in the doorway of the barn was blocked as Sam appeared around the corner. Both horse and young woman had been so lost in reverie in the musty quiet of the barn that they jumped simultaneously. Pru, genuinely alarmed this time, stepped on the side of the bucket, sending the water arcing in a perfect wave onto Lisl, plastering her hair to her head and her clothes to her body.

"Whoa there, girl," Sam said in a soothing voice to Pru, as he leaned over to right the bucket. "Sorry to surprise, you, ladies; Lisl, are you ready to wrap Pru's hoof?"

She nodded assent, gathered her wits about her, and went to the medicine rack in the tack room to fetch the supplies they needed. Coming back with gauze, a roll of duct tape, scissors, and antiseptic cream, she set them down on an empty burlap feed bag while Sam persuaded Pru that she had to go back into her three-legged stance.

Once Sam, who was facing Pru's rear end, was able to cradle the huge hoof in his hands, Lisl moved in facing Sam. She applied the curry-yellow ointment to the soft, rotten spot in Pru's abscessed hoof and unwound the first long length of gauze. She worked swiftly, knowing the weight of that hoof on Sam's back.

Their heads inches from each other, bodies bent over their work, Sam felt a sudden rush of tenderness for Lisl. He had always admired her competence and agility, and the open confidence with which she looked at life; but suddenly, with a stab that hit so hard it took his breath away, he envied her youth and freedom, and he wanted her as he had never wanted anything in his life.

Lisl's T-shirt hung over her shorts, adhering to her high, small breasts; and her upper torso swung in a tight circle following her hands as she peeled the duct tape around the horse's hoof to encase the gauze.

He noticed her capable hands, the skin unblemished from the sun, the nails cut straight across; he marveled at how the sunlight picked out the slight blond fuzz on her forearms and the deathly white of her inner thigh as she knelt, one knee on the gunny sack, the other up and forward for balance. He was mesmerized by the gold of her straight hair, normally tucked behind her ears, but which now fell forward like a veil, leaving the supple curve of her neck bare as she concentrated on her work.

Something must have made her aware of the intensity of his gaze—for he was consuming her visually—and she raised her head to look at him. As she did so, a strand of wet hair stayed plastered across her face; and, in a movement that summed up all of the yearning within him, he shifted the weight of Pru's leg onto one hand and reached out with the other to free the hair.

Midway in the short space between them, his brain contradicted his heart, and his hand hesitated in mid-air. Before he could withdraw it, Lisl, with the certainty that characterized her every move, caught it, turned the palm towards her, and, without taking her eyes off his face, slowly kissed the inside of his cupped hand.

In pain from his desire as she let go of his hand, he took care to set Pru's bandaged foot squarely down on the ground. Freed, he looked down at Lisl. She hadn't stirred from her position, nor had she stopped looking at him. He closed the space between them, raised her to her feet by the shoulders, simultaneously turning her until her back was against Pru's bulk, and followed through with his original intent by tucking the hair on both sides of her face behind her ears.

As he did so, his eyes questioned her, and she answered simply, wordlessly, by pulling her shirt over her head and letting it drop on the gunnysack.

Her bold submission was so direct that he felt as if he were swimming in a thick sea of gratitude and desire. Making his desire wait on his gratitude, he reached for both her hands lying quietly at her side, and, entwining his fingers with hers, lifted her arms, bent at the elbow, until they were pinned by his against Pru's warm, permissive body. Wordlessly, he thanked her.

Later, lying on the pile of horse blankets in the stall to which he had carried her when they were no longer able to slow the pace of their lovemaking, he realized that never in his life had he had an inkling of the layers of pleasure to be gotten from the act of love.

This, he realized, was because this time he had given as much as he had gotten. He knew that he had physically touched Lisl in ways that were new to her, and her clear pleasure and thirst for more had released him to explore that thirst without asking for permission or apologizing after the fact. Her lithe, spare body had shown him the way and welcomed him.

She had loosed the ties of worry, failure, and isolation that with each year had seemed to more tightly circumscribe his life. He felt reamed out, purged, miraculously emptied.

All that stood between them, the ways in which this act had complicated their lives, the hurt it would cause, how they would get through the next few days—all these were like the dust mites filtering slowly downwards in the sunlight outside the stall above Pru's dozing head; silently there, yet seeming not to exist around them in the shade of the stall.

Lisl lay on her side facing him, her head on her arm, her legs spread eagled to catch any breeze that might be stirring, eyes shut as if to keep out reality. She felt the caress of Sam's finger running across the bones of her face, felt his eyes warm her body.

"Hans, poor Hans," she said, almost in a whisper.

"You can't marry out of pity," she heard him say, answering this non-question.

"No worse than marrying out of necessity," she shot back, taking some of the sting out of her words by moving in to burrow her head between his cheek and shoulder. He heard a choking sound and then, with lips against his neck, she moaned, "What will we do? I hate messes, I hate them."

This was so un-Lisl-like, this asking for solutions that didn't exist, that he wasn't surprised to feel her tears on his neck. Raising her face so that he could see it, he said, "I don't honestly know right now; but I do know we have to put on a ride, and a good one at that. After it's over we will have to... have to..." his voice trailed off.

Suddenly the burden of the farm, the horses, the guests, Elsie—oh God, Elsie—landed back in his consciousness, and he finished with "deal with it." The spell had been broken, and with no more words they rose, put on their clothes, and left the barn, as if walking away from a dream.

FOUR

LISL RAISED THE LEVER OF THE WATER spigot outside the house, and leaning down, splashed the earth-cooled water onto her face again and again, as if water could somehow wash away the complexity that had suddenly replaced the assumptions she had taken for granted about her life.

She felt no sense of moral wrongdoing; in her mind the action that she, after all, had initiated had so overwhelmed her—at the moment of decision when she had caught Sam's hand in midair—that the very intensity of feeling represented to her a kind of cosmic permission. She was not religious, but she recognized the spiritual in others, in herself, and in the natural world, and knew that she had just taken on a monstrous power to wound.

The church's dictum "Thou shalt not commit adultery" she could recognize as applying to her in this case, despite the fact that she was not married; but the mere exchange of vows seemed to her less binding than the accrued longing that had washed over them both. She felt no guilt for this. What gave her an increasing sense of foreboding was the inevitability of hurting Hans and Elsie, both of whom she loved and whom she knew depended upon her.

Without knowing it, Hans and Elsie were like civilians caught in the crossfire of a military engagement: innocent, unarmed, blindsided. And it had all happened so fast. She had imagined that if the world turned upside down that it would happen at a pace that she could adjust to and cope with, maybe even helping others to do the same. How vain!

The events of today shot her into the unfamiliar orbit of being the problem rather than the problem solver. Her choices were stark: she could deny the strongest force she had ever felt, or she could follow it, causing heartbreak and, in the process, permanently changing lives.

She felt an absurd fit of pique at the quicksilver speed with which it had all come about. Thank goodness Hans was to stay behind and take care of the farm when they took out the riders; she didn't think she could have borne it otherwise. Perhaps in a few days she could do a better job of separating out duty from joy, love from pleasure. Being Swiss, she swept her bewilderment aside and lost herself in the work of preparation for the ride.

As Elsie and Hans were turning into the farm road on the way back from Waynesboro, from the other direction a car flew by them, braked suddenly after passing the Whiskey Ridge Farm sign, reversed itself, and then followed them up to the house. It turned out to be Stanley and Lenore Gibson, with Lenore at the wheel, anxious to get to the farm in time to spend the afternoon learning about the horse operation.

Aiming to avoid introductions, Hans jumped out of the truck, grabbed several grocery bags at once, and shot for the porch door. Lenore and Stanley emerged from their car and introduced themselves to Elsie, who called nervously for Sam. Simultaneously Sam came from the house and Lisl from the smokehouse, converging on the guests and the truck at the same time.

"Welcome to Whiskey Ridge," boomed Sam, vigorously shaking their hands. "We've got a great riding trip set up for you, and you've arrived in plenty of time to settle in and tour the farm. Lisl Perrin here knows almost as much about it as

I do, so I'll get her to show you to your rooms while we get these groceries in. When you're ready, come on down to the porch for some iced tea or a cold one." He winked at Stanley, who had their suitcases in tow.

"Sounds good," said Lenore, a vigorous, direct woman in her mid-forties, as she grabbed their riding helmets and boots from the trunk of the car, slammed it down with her elbow and followed her husband and Lisl into the house.

While Lisl showed them to the master bedroom, Hans and Sam emptied the back of the truck and unwrapped the cold cuts on the kitchen counter, rolling pieces of bread around a few slices and hurriedly eating them as they stowed the groceries. Elsie detoured to her little herb garden in the whiskey half-barrel outside the porch door for sprigs of mint for the iced tea, leaving the tea and four bottles of beer on the porch table.

Then she set to work on their supper. As Elsie was moving her chopping board to the center of the counter and arranging the cabbages around it, Lenore came through the kitchen on the way to the porch. Seeing what Elsie was about to do, she moved towards her, asking, "Would you like some help with that?"

Worried that Lenore would be shocked at the wormholes in the cabbages, she answered over her shoulder, "No, thanks, I think Sam will be wanting to show you the horses," and with that bent her head to the job at hand.

Four o'clock was approaching, the hour when they were all to assemble to go down to the barn, but the Lapsleys and Sarah Feldcamp had not shown up yet. The Lapsleys had called from Charlottesville, where they were eating lunch, saying they had underestimated the time it took to drive from Washington and that they would be a half-hour or so late in arriving.

Sarah Feldcamp, who was coming the farthest of any of them, had yet to be heard from. Stanley, obviously in no hurry to attach himself to a horse, had settled into the hammock strung between the honey locusts beside the house, and was lost in his reading.

Lenore, iced tea in hand, was peppering Lisl with questions—where was she from in Switzerland, what kind of an exchange program had she come over on, was she having visa problems, how did she happen to speak such good English?

To the last question, Lisl, too diplomatic to blurt out that only the American educational system does not require proficiency in another language for graduation, responded lightly, "This is my third trip here, and working with people who don't speak your language is the very best way to learn a new one."

Lenore cocked her head at Lisl and asked, "That young man I saw earlier, is he your boyfriend?" No sooner was the question out of her mouth than she backtracked, "I'm sorry, I shouldn't have asked you such a personal question. My curiosity always gets me in trouble."

"I don't mind," said Lisl. "The answer to your question is, yes, he's my boyfriend. Always has been, actually." She paused, wondering whether or not to go farther and explain to this curious American about the bizarre intersection of their two childhoods, hers and Hans's.

Although they had known each other only a few minutes, Lisl felt drawn to Lenore, and on impulse decided to tell her their story. She had told Elsie and Sam about Hans at the end of her first summer with them. Somehow she welcomed the thought of this confident, friendly woman twice her age knowing why she was there and what decision she had come there to make.

Her mind, she realized, had exiled to the far reaches of her consciousness what had happened in the barn this very morning, as if by sheer mental exertion she could take reality back to the simplicity of yesterday.

"We were next-door neighbors," she started in, "in the small town of Serneus, which hangs off the slope of a mountain alongside the narrow-gauge railway that takes hikers and skiers further up to the town of Klosters, in German-speaking Switzerland. My father worked for the railroad and Mother worked in a bakery in town. Hans's parents ran a herd of cows on the slopes beneath the village.

"One spring night when we were four years old, a freezing rain turned the road up from the valley into sheet ice. Hans's parents were driving home, coming up the mountain, when the car they were in veered out of control and struck a tree, killing them both instantly. Hans is an only child, and neither of his parents had any siblings, so Hans has no aunts or uncles.

"I was the youngest of five children close in age; even before Hans's parents were killed, Hans had spent most of his time in the cheerful bedlam of our house. I can't remember a time when Hans was not right beside me.

"Even though we lived in a small house full to overflowing, with my four brothers crowded into a room for two and me in a room that had formerly been a closet, Mother and Father adopted Hans. The very night of his parents' death, unaware at his age of the significance of what had happened, he could sense that the adults were upset and was comforted by sleeping in the bed with me, as he had so many times before. Hans became my own private playmate, my defender when my older brothers ignored or teased me.

"For Hans, I was sister, mother, and closest friend; and when the time came for school, I took up the added role of helping him with his studies, which came more easily for me than for him. My parents laughingly referred to us as Siamese twins, since we seemed to move as one, even down to sharing food crazes. For a solid year we ate little besides Nutella spread on toast. We shared an imaginary world peopled by characters unknown to the rest of the family. Hans and I drove my brothers mad, as we could play for hours, oblivious to their noise and games."

"Why didn't your parents move Hans into the boys'

room?" interrupted Lenore, engrossed in Lisl's story. "A room that is too small for four might as well be too small for five, especially if it's boys."

"They tried when Hans reached school age," answered Lisl, "but each morning they would find that he had crept back into bed with me. Anyway, my brothers didn't want him in their crowded quarters and so they told him horror stories to scare him.

"Also," Lisl admitted, "I had nightmares sleeping alone, which woke the whole house. After several weeks of rough nights, my parents gave up, and Hans moved back in with me.

"Five years later, before adolescence set in and after two of the older boys had moved out of the house, Hans was again moved into the boys' room. This lasted for three years, and in no way affected the sixteen hours of the day that we still managed to spend together."

From the porch came Sam's voice, "Lenore, would you mind moving your car over behind the smokehouse? It can stay there while you're away."

"Sure," she said, and to Lisl, "Hold on, hold on, I want to hear the rest of this. I'll be right back."

In Lenore's absence Lisl's mind went over what she didn't have to explain. What she and Hans needed to find out for themselves about sex, they had found out together, in the cow herders' sheds that dotted the slopes beneath the village.

Neither was shy with the other, and, after initial awkward fumblings, the sex act seemed a celebration of the new realm their bodies had discovered, like an unexpected hidden gift found long after the Christmas tree had been taken down. To them it had seemed as natural and unspoiled as the seductive summer warmth that made them languid in their exploration of each other.

Her mother had realized the change the first day that they came home after discovering this new realm. She was a realistic woman who, after all, had not bothered to get married until after the first two boys had been born. Her chief concern had been that Lisl not become pregnant, ruin her chances to continue her schooling, and feel locked into getting married when she was still virtually a child. She made sure that Lisl took birth control pills, and the obvious was recognized when Hans, for the second time, moved back into her room when they were both sixteen.

Lenore, hurrying back and sliding into the chair next to her, interrupted Lisl's memories. "Do go on," she prompted, turning an expectant face towards Lisl.

"I guess it was pre-ordained that we would become a pair," continued Lisl. "Our schoolmates expected it, and so did my family, even my brothers."

"Oh," sighed Lenore, clapping her hands together, "this is a Swiss fairy tale!" Lisl managed a small smile at the unwitting irony of Lenore's statement.

She went on, "My first summer as an exchange student in Virginia, when we were seventeen, was the first time we had been separated. Hans stayed in Serneus, apprenticed to the local blacksmith in order to learn his trade. The second summer, when Sam and Elsie had come up with the money for my plane trip back to Virginia, Hans tried unsuccessfully to persuade me to take a summer job working in one of the hotels in Klosters that caters to hikers in the summertime.

"Once I returned after that second summer, Hans complained that I talked about Sam and Elsie and their farm in Virginia as if I were a family member. For the first time I think he felt left out of my world, threatened, somehow vulnerable. When he tried to express his worry, I'd say that he must come with me to see what appealed to me so, and then he would understand, and that it would appeal to him, too. I set aside part of my law firm salary to pay for his ticket."

Her voice drifted off just as the sound of a car motor shifting down on the turn around the barn penetrated through the open window.

"That must be the Lapsleys," they heard Sam say from

the other room as he headed out the door to greet them. A few minutes later he returned, leading a couple that looked to be in that long stretch of years between middle and old age. Meg Lapsley had two pairs of chaps hanging over her arm and carried their hard hats in her other hand. She kept her curly brown hair off her face behind a blue kerchief tied at the nape of her neck, and her expectant expression looked the very picture of someone who was finally on vacation.

Her husband, Will, turned sideways to squeeze through the door with their two duffels, holding one in front of himself and one behind.

"Greetings, all," he managed to get out as he kept moving across the porch toward the hall with his load. "Meg, what have you got in here, bowling balls?"

Lisl hurried to get ahead of him to show the way to Sam's mother's old room so he could put the bags down.

Meg paid no attention to his question, but dropped the things she was carrying on the back of a chair and introduced herself to her fellow riders and their hosts. Lenore explained that she was taking the ride for the dual purposes of having fun and writing an article on it, and when she found that Meg was both a writer and a horseback rider, they fell into conversation.

"I'm so glad," said Meg, "that it's you and not me writing it up; I don't have to keep notes or remember things minute to minute. All I'm here for is to enjoy myself!"

Will returned empty-handed and shook hands all around, his boyish face a bit of a shock when matched with his mature frame. He had a generous smile and a natural ease in his greeting that made it clear that people were his business.

To Elsie, who had momentarily stopped chopping in order to say hello and was standing at the kitchen counter with knife still in hand, he joked, "Oh, I hope you're going to use that on the vegetables and not on me!" as he came over to shake her other hand. Elsie said nothing, but looked up at him quickly to check that he was joking and gave him a half-smile.

Sam, failing to hide his annoyance and speaking to no one in particular, said, "Don't expect her to get the joke." Elsie didn't look at him, and for a few moments there was an awkward silence as the guests took in the new edginess in the room.

Sam, trying to fill the void, noted that they were still minus Sarah. "We'll give her another hour, since I hate repeating myself. I'll look for you all to show up at the barn at five o'clock sharp, dressed in your riding clothes and ready to learn how we do business around here. Meanwhile Lisl and I will be getting your horses in from the pasture. Lenore, why don't you come with us? It'll give me a chance to tell you about our operation."

"I'd like to do that," Lenore answered, "just let me grab my notebook and pencil."

Meg and Will opted to catch a quick nap after agreeing to meet at five. In their bedroom they took off their shoes so as not to dirty the quilt, and then lay down on the old-fashioned double bed.

"Ooouf," went Will as his body hit the unyielding surface of a horsehair mattress, "this is going to be a long night!"

"Sssssshhh," cautioned Meg, "we don't want them to hear us complaining."

"I don't give a damn if they do hear us," replied Will. "Sleeping in this bed for one night is going to make our three nights camping seem like the lap of luxury. And what's all this about no screens in the windows; are we going to be eaten alive by mosquitoes as well?"

"If we don't turn on the lights in here, we won't be," said Meg, masking her chagrin as she had made all the plans for this vacation. Hearing no more, she looked over with fondness at the closed eyes and open mouth of her sleeping husband.

An hour later they were gathered in the aisle of the barn, watching Sam demonstrate the proper way to saddle a horse. They would be using western saddles that hung on racks in the tack room, across from the bridles hanging neatly under each horse's nameplate.

Sam was standing next to Sassafras, a mare who was always a favorite with guests. She had been named for the tree she had been born under, and, like its leaves, she herself was a bit loopy and oversized. There was something innately comical about her build: somehow all her parts didn't connect properly, but she had an easygoing temperament.

Sam was in the midst of showing them that, unlike the main girth, the stabilizing rear girth on a western saddle should not be cinched tightly, when Sarah Feldcamp slipped quietly into their midst, trying not to interrupt the lesson.

"Young lady," snapped Sam, "I hope this is the only time you'll be late. In the next few days we'll be riding over some beautiful but difficult terrain, and for your own safety and that of your horse you will need to pay close attention to what you're told. This is not a joy ride we're taking. I've been doing these rides for ten years and I haven't had an accident yet, and don't intend to start now."

"I'm so sorry," said Sarah, her face pinched and earnest. "I turned the wrong way on the bypass around Charlottesville and was halfway to Richmond before I figured out what I'd done wrong." Sarah was a young woman in her late twenties who would have been prettier had she not had a skin problem on her face that had left some scarring.

Lenore stepped towards Sarah, holding out her hand, "Don't worry, we had just started, you didn't miss much. My name is Lenore Gibson, and this is my husband, Stanley."

This eased the situation somewhat and allowed for introductions to be made all around. While this was going on, Lisl spoke quietly to Sam. When the guests brought their attention back to the horse, Sam was nowhere to be seen, and Lisl was holding a bridle in one hand and scratching Sassy's ear with the other.

In fact, it looked as if Sassy was rubbing Lisl; the horse was so content with the impromptu massage that she leaned the entire top of her head against the pressure of Lisl's hand, her tongue lolling outside her mouth in a fit of contentment and her eyes rolled back in her head.

"Stop, you silly girl," laughed Lisl, "I can't show these nice people how to put on your bridle unless you stop your comedy act." When Lisl removed her hand, Sassy, off- balance, looked aggrieved, making everyone laugh.

"Most of you know this routine," said Lisl, "but no one has done it recently, and Stanley, you may never have done it. The important thing is to station yourself on the left side of the horse's head, put the reins over the neck, and face yourself and the bridle in the direction the horse is headed.

"Hold the top of the bridle in one hand and the bit in the other, and urge the horse to accept the bit by gently sliding the thumb of your hand into the top corner of the horse's mouth—don't worry, there are no teeth back there to chomp down on your thumb.

"When the bit is in the mouth, settle the top of the bridle over the ears. Just move slowly and don't get anxious, or you will transfer that anxiety to the horse. If it doesn't work the first time, wait a little bit and try again. Don't force it. Remember, a horse is so much bigger than you are that it will always win a battle of strength."

"I haven't bridled a horse in a while, Lisl, may I try it?" Sarah stepped forward at Lisl's affirming nod, took the bridle in both hands as instructed and, with Sassy bored but obliging, managed to get it on.

"That's good, Sarah, but remember she has two ears, and this band here," Lisl indicated by slipping it over the ear on the far side, "must go on, too. If you need to, come around this side to do it."

By this time, Sam had rounded up horses for each of the riders and tied them by their halters to a ring in the wall of their stall. He came back up the aisle to where they were standing.

"I've picked a horse for each of you," he began. "I'll tell you a little about them, and then with our help you can tack them up and bring them out in front of the barn where you can use the mounting block to get on. When we're on the trip, you'll need to find a tree stump, a fence, or one of us to give you a leg up. Then you can ride a little in the ring to see if I've made good matches, horses to people."

FIVE

SAM HAD A SIXTH SENSE WHEN it came to matching people to horses, even before he had seen them ride. One of the reasons riders loved his camping trips was that his horses were well trained and well suited to dealing with the mountain terrain. For years members of the Virginia General Assembly had come up to Whiskey Ridge Farm in groups of fifteen to go on all-day rides in the foothills of the Blue Ridge. This was a nearly all-male group, and Sam slipped easily into their back-slapping, tobacco-chewing, joke-telling camaraderie. He also made sure that in each horse's saddlebags was a dollop of bourbon to go along with the picnic lunch.

Sarah asked if she could ride Sassafras and was thrilled when the answer was yes. They spent more time in the ring together than anyone else, and very soon it was as if they were old friends. Sarah had brought some green June apples with her when she came, and had been doling them out to secure her friendship with Sassy before the ride began.

Will Lapsley was assigned a large gelding named Geronimo. He had a big head, kind eyes, and large, expressive ears that rotated around like antennae. Geronimo was a gentle giant, with a long stride and a willing attitude. He was young, only five years old, and for the first three years of his life he had been turned out in the pasture without much attention.

As a result he had a bad habit. He was easy to catch, as he was a sucker for carrots and apples, but sometimes when he was being led he would decide he would rather be elsewhere, use his size to jerk the lead line out of the hands of the person leading him, and trot over to examine whatever had interested him. He never strayed far; a fistful of oats would bring him trotting in, lead rope swinging to and fro as if to say, "I'll cooperate most of the time, but don't ask me to give up my independence."

This quirk was described to Will, who said he could deal with it. When Sam turned his attention to Meg, Will picked up a brush and began grooming Geronimo while the big horse nobbled his pockets, looking for carrots.

Meg had ridden all her life and loved lively horses, so Sam assigned her a mare that was on the small side. She had a proud head and a more nervous temperament than the other horses, but her gaits were extraordinarily smooth and comfortable.

"What's her name?" asked Meg.

"Lady Mischief," replied Sam, "because she mostly acts like a lady but isn't above the occasional mischief." Meg looked pleased and straight away began to introduce herself to the alert animal in front of her.

Sam pointed Lenore toward Challenger, the best-looking horse of the lot. Challenger was tired of waiting and had pawed the straw and dirt out from under where he was tied in the stall. He looked at Lenore as if to say, "Let's get on with it," as she approached.

Lisl led the slow-moving, big-footed Packer up to the guests.

"Stanley," said Sam, "This is truly my most bombproof horse. In fact, it might take a bomb to get him to trot!" At this, Stanley's mildly anxious expression relaxed into a smile.

While the others tacked up their mounts under Sam's vigilant eye, Lisl helped Stanley with his preparations.

"Your best position, Stanley, will be sandwiched in the middle of the riders. Packer is a follower, not a leader, happiest when his nose and tail are inches from the horses in front of and behind him." Lisl's quiet, knowledgeable manner settled Stanley's nerves and soon he was on board and circling the ring happily.

Once again, Sam's matchmaking abilities seemed to have paid off, as all five guests were happy with his choices. After a half-hour of feeling out their mounts in the ring, they hung their tack back in the barn and turned the horses out for the evening. Walking back up the hill to the house, there was good-humored banter about creaky knees and sore rear ends, but Sam felt relieved that there didn't seem to be anyone on the trip who was not up to it.

At dusk they sat out on the screened porch. Hans and Sam stuck to beer; Lisl had nothing to drink, while the guests took Elsie up on her offer of mint juleps. Elsie had drawn the dog-haired coverings off of the old sofa and armchairs on the porch. Meg and Will sank into the sofa and immediately wondered how they were going to get out again. Lenore and Stanley slipped into the armchairs, and Lisl and Hans sat on an ottoman back to back, supporting each other. Sam brought in two plastic chairs from the yard, although Elsie seldom lit on hers, preferring to busy herself in the kitchen. The porch protected them from the mosquitoes that had multiplied during the intermittent rains of the last several weeks.

"It's either floods or droughts around here," exclaimed Sam. "Five years ago, in a drought that came on slowly over the course of the summer, one of the springs that gravity-feed the house and the barn went dry. The small pond in the cattle pasture shriveled down to a hole with stagnant water in it. There was a thin film of weeds sprouting in the dirt where the pond had been, and the Herefords—who are used to standing belly-deep in the water on a hot day—stared down into the crater, trying to figure it out." Looking down at the porch floor, he mimed the uncomprehending face of a cow.

Elsie remembered that awful summer, and in her mind's eye saw again the cows ranged along the fence line when grass in their pasture was stiff and gray, twisting their necks like cooked spaghetti in order to push their heads sideways through the strands of wire fencing to reach the tufts of un-eaten grass on the other side. "Luther's Creek stopped running altogether," reminisced Sam, "the water pooled between rocks, and there were gaps of parched creek bed between the pools."

"We stopped using the indoor bathtub; instead, we hosed ourselves down in the darkness outside before we went to bed, and flushed the toilet with buckets filled at the kitchen sink before the water ran hot enough to wash the dishes."

"I remember your telling me," chimed in Lisl, "that laundromats in Waynesboro shut down and restaurants started using paper plates."

"Here at the farm we stopped listening to the radio because there was nothing on but news of the drought," Sam said. "Maybe this was news to city folk, but not to us. The weather column in the *Waynesboro Virginian* had a five-day forecast made up of small symbols for sunshine, clouds and rain. Every day the symbol for sun was in the first four columns and the symbol for rain filled up the fifth column. Every day rain was just four days off, but it never arrived. I figured the weatherman must have a perverse sense of humor."

"Now we've got the opposite problem," said Lisl, "rain, mud and swollen creeks. But at least things are green and beautiful, which sometimes isn't the case around here in August."

Sarah, the last to arrive, had been listening to the radio on her trip to the farm. "Speaking of the weather," she hesitantly began, "I heard on the news driving down here that hundreds of hippies had a very wet weekend in Woodstock, New York. They were supposed to be listening to music, but there were lots of anti-Vietnam War speeches, and lots of arrests for smoking pot. There was so much rain that tents were afloat and so many people that food ran out. So many more people came than any of the organizers had imagined."

Picking up steam, she went on. "They mentioned that Camille, the hurricane that was stalled in the Gulf of Mexico, has changed direction and now looks like it will hit the Gulf Coast instead of the Florida panhandle. They are evacuating the coastal areas today."

As Sarah reported what she knew about Camille, Sam flicked on the television, as much out of idle interest to see just how bad things could get on the Gulf Coast as to search for a hint as to whether or not they might encounter a backlash from the hurricane on their ride.

Evacuations had been underway since that morning, the announcer said, all along the Mississippi Gulf coast, with Biloxi and Gulfport radio stations abandoning regular programming so that announcements about the mandatory evacuation could take its place. Hurricane warnings now included all of southeastern Louisiana as well. Gale-force winds extended out from the eye of the hurricane 200 miles in all directions, indicating that its swath of destruction could be huge once it made landfall.

Unbeknownst to them, that afternoon Air Force pilots in a C-130 had penetrated the eye of Camille, and what they saw there they had never seen before. The co-pilot wrote in his report, "Instead of the green and white splotches normally found in a storm, the sea surface was in deep furrows running along the wind direction. The velocity was far beyond the descriptions used in our training." He recorded a very low barometric pressure reading of 26.62 inches of mercury. Although he estimated that Camille's winds were 190 miles an hour, he could not stick around to verify that horrifying figure as the plane lost an engine, and their attention turned to safely negotiating the way back to Ellington Air Force Base. That Sunday afternoon's reconnaissance flight turned out to be the last flight into the eye of Camille.

But none of the riders sitting on Sam and Elsie's screened porch knew any of this. What was clear, however, was that by the time Camille made landfall, it would be a Category 5 hurricane. Hearing this, Meg Lapsley shuddered and said, "Times like this, I'm so grateful to be in the center of central Virginia and nowhere near a coastline!"

"Oh yeah," responded Sam, "and those announcers love nothing better than to terrorize their listeners. They always exaggerate." Happy to be so far removed, they finished their drinks and had supper in the gloaming of a late-summer evening, their thoughts miles away from the pending disaster on the Gulf Coast.

While Hans was helping Elsie with the dishes, each rider got down on the floor and followed Sam's precise instructions rolling their packs that the two packhorses would carry in addition to the food and cooking gear. Each laid out a large brown oilcloth tarp, unzipped their sleeping bag until it lay open on top of the tarp, laid their pajamas, extra shirt, socks and underwear in the canvas bag they'd been given, put that on top of the sleeping bag, and then rolled up the whole package and secured it with bungee cords.

Lisl was on her knees helping Meg, who was slow to get the hang of rolling and securing the tarp so that it would stay closed as it bounced along on the side of a packhorse. Sam gave orders and impatiently stepped around the prone bodies, disbelieving that such a simple procedure could take so long, and occasionally leaning over and just finishing the job.

By bedtime the guests were all relieved to retreat to their rooms. Sarah was a good sport about her curtained alcove off the living room and the downstairs bath she shared with Elsie, Sam, Lisl, and Hans, who had to come back in the house to use the facilities. The Gibsons and the Lapsleys shared the upstairs bath with its Victorian claw-footed tub, a solitary sentry standing by the window. No shower, Will thought to himself, as he and Meg peeked into the room on the way to bed. Reading his thought, Meg whispered, "This is true luxury compared to what you're going to get when we're camping tomorrow night!"

"Jeez, don't remind me," he whispered back.

Elsie and Lisl were in the kitchen, with Lisl reading off the checklist of items they needed for Elsie to pack. The Dutch oven, heavy iron fry pan, and metal coffee maker clanked down in a big Army duffel bag, along with the tin cups, plates and cutlery, which nested within each other in separate plastic bags.

The perishables would go in a cooler early the next day. The first night's meal would be the best, since the ice would last long enough for local trout to be the feature of that meal. Sam gave the women a wide berth as he packed the Coleman stove, its fuel, and lanterns.

Every second of the evening, Lisl had been acutely aware of where Sam was, who he was talking to, what he was doing. She felt as if she were in the room with a working electric fence, and she tried to position herself so as to avoid shock.

The others were there only as backdrop; she could answer their questions and smile politely while doing so, but all the while there was a pounding in her ears that was so loud it was disorienting, and she felt the awkward heaviness of longing. She had realized, since that morning, that Hans was more her brother than her own natural brothers. She had mistaken sexual intimacy for passion, tenderness and protectiveness for the naked vulnerability of love.

And whose fault was this, she thought? No one's fault, really. She and Hans had just taken the laziest route into adulthood. Their closeness meant that they stood together against the barbed comments of fellow students, the intrusiveness of teachers, the scrutiny of her parents. They had been married in all but name. She sickened at the thought that she had allowed a door to shut on her life, even as she saw that if there were fault to be assigned, most of it would go to her.

In their relationship, Hans and Lisl had never had the dangerous give and take of leading sometimes and sometimes being led. Encouraged by both nature and nurture, Hans was a follower, which she had taken for granted and, by leading, reinforced. She knew herself to be tougher than Hans. As a child, when her brothers would decide to make her mad by ordering her around, she would barrel into them, flailing away with her small fists, kicking their shins and biting any piece of skin she could get hold of with her teeth.

This entertained her brothers mightily, which would make her even madder. Their punishment, if Hans and their parents were out, was to hold her down on the ironing board in the basement and give her what they called "the rough treatment." This consisted of tickling her, pulling her nose, and giving her "cabbage ears," rubbing her ears so hard that they were beet red and stuck out. She never once told on them, as it would have just made matters worse.

She was standing four steps down the basement stairs, searching for extra batteries for the flashlights, feeling along the shelf of the unfinished wall in the weak light when Sam came around the corner at the bottom of the stairs. He was carrying a canister of fuel in each hand, but when he saw her he put down the canisters on the lowest step and took the basement stairs two at a time until he stood behind her on the narrow staircase.

Lisl had frozen in position the moment she saw him. Sam moved his body into the curve of her own; he carefully put his arm along her extended arm, curling his fingers around her own, gently folding her arms against her body so that she was enlisted in molding herself to him. She felt his chin resting on her right shoulder, his breath in her ear. With his nose he traced the outline of her earlobe. Paralyzed, she felt his kisses, light and teasing, on her neck and along her jaw on the right side of her face.

Feeling as if she were drowning, she arched away from him, willing herself up the stairway with the batteries and back into the world of her responsibilities. Once back on the first floor, she busied herself with preparations for the morning until she was sure Hans would have given up waiting for her return and fallen asleep. Elsie was the last to go to bed. Late that night she was sitting at her desk, shoulders hunched forward, using the midnight quiet to pay farm bills that could be put off no longer.

SIX

MORNING BROUGHT THE SAME WEAK SUNSHINE that had characterized most of August, unusual for late summer in this part of the upper South. Normally the worst heat of the season came between mid-July and mid-August, bringing with it days of relentless humidity and very little rain. The current muddy conditions on the farm were more like early June.

Lisl was unable to sleep, lying next to Hans's warm bulk. He slept deeply and well, ignorant of the seismic shifts going on around him.

Lying there, she tried to use her rational mind to see her way forward, but rationality kept butting up against what one owed a person that had been so much a part of your life. And this line of thinking was not even dealing with the larger, looming heartbreak of Elsie and Sam.

When her tired body did occasionally have its way, she drifted in a close-to-consciousness, dream-churned sleep. From time to time she could pull herself out of it, but then, too quickly, it would claim her again. Odd, but there were no people in her dreams, just a totally emptied Whiskey Ridge Farm. The pasture with no horses in it, the house abandoned with holes in the roof and panes missing from windows, the vegetable garden overgrown by a towering mass of autumn olive trees randomly planted, and birds—birds flying into and out of the pane-less windows and stripping the garden of its summer plenty.

Strangest of all amidst this devastation, there were certain simple wrongs that had been righted. The apple trees were in a luxuriant bloom that defied their old age, and the brass dachshund boot scrapper by the back stoop had been mended; it sat, upright and polished, ready for boot scraping—but whose boots? The collapsed television antenna on top of the roof was gone, replaced by a shiny weathervane, whirling insanely on a windless day.

Lisl woke before daylight, disoriented and played out, got up and dressed in the dark, and went into the house to get breakfast going. Only coffee, she thought to herself, had a chance of clearing the webs of confusion and loss in her head. She put the percolator on high boil, flipped on the radio, started the sausage cooking, and fetched apples from their storage bin on the porch.

Lisl was soothed by the repetitive work of cutting around the core of the apples and then chopping the sections for fried apples that would go well with the sausage for a celebratory send-off breakfast. A glance at the back door, where Sam's mud boots were missing, told her that he was already down at the barn feeding the horses. Before long Lenore appeared, energetic and businesslike, and looking well rested. She seemed happy to find only Lisl at work in the kitchen. Without being asked, she, too, found a knife and began helping with the apples.

Lenore was intrigued by this slip of a young woman, so perceptive and so mature for her age. Instinctively she felt drawn to her, and still curious about the picture Lisl had painted of her childhood with Hans.

"Lisl," she asked as they worked together in the wan light of the new day, "what brought you to Virginia in the first place? Sam tells me you had no experience with horses before coming here but that you are a natural with them and also a quick study with anything that interests you.

"How could you learn to ride so quickly when you hadn't been exposed to horses as a child? I never skied until I was in my twenties, and although I love being outside all day and drinking in the beauty around me, I don't think I'll ever ski right down into the fall line the way expert skiers do. Maybe I'm just gutless, but I like to think that kind of grace comes from skiing in childhood, before fear of the pitch of a slope kicks in. Also, how come your English is so good?"

They both laughed as Lenore drew breath and Lisl responded, "No wonder you are a journalist, you have so many questions!"

"It's true," answered Lenore, "journalists are just glorified busybodies. But I really am interested."

"It's quite simple, really," said Lisl, deciding to deal with Lenore's questions backwards. "The smaller the country in Europe, the more languages its citizens learn in school. Switzerland is the size of an overgrown national park. Depending on which canton we come from, we grow up speaking either French or German and understanding the other. Our livelihoods depend upon learning good English. Tourism is our biggest industry.

"After I was introduced to horses," she continued, "I realized almost immediately that I wanted to work with them, even before I had learned to ride. Horses are as individualistic as people. You can divine a person's characteristics by listening closely to what they say, but to divine a horse's personality you are dependent on your other senses, which used together become a sort of sixth horse sense.

"You can smell rotting material in a horse's hoof, you can see the beginning of colic in the restless way they move, you can feel along a horse's vertebrae for a tender spot or along the leg for heat in a joint. Most of all you have to be constantly interpreting what you see: ears that suddenly rotate backwards, dull eyes, the way a horse holds its head. There's just no end to it, and sometimes you never know if you are a hundred percent right, fifty percent right, or just plain wrong.

"I came here the first time as a lark, to see the States, make some money, do something independent of my family. No grand plans. But this time the idea is to see if Hans also could adjust to living in the States, working as a blacksmith and as a farm manager. Initially I was hopeful, but it may be wishful thinking...." Her voice trailed off.

Lenore had come to this conclusion as well, but didn't think it would add anything if she weighed in. Instead she asked, "Do you mind if I quote you in my article, that bit about a sixth horse sense?"

"Not at all," answered Lisl.

Just then the screen door slammed as Elsie hurried into the kitchen looking flustered, and then sighed with relief when she saw that Lisl had started preparing breakfast.

"I overslept, it was so dark in the shed," which was more than Lenore had heard her say since she arrived.

"Don't worry," said Lisl, "the apples and sausage are on. Just make your famous batter bread and we're in business. The oven is preheated and the butter is melting in the pan."

Quickly Elsie blanched the white corn meal in boiling water, added the milk, eggs, salt and baking powder, and used an electric beater to add the butter melted in the cast iron pan Lisl removed from the oven. Within five minutes they were a half-hour away from a sinfully good Virginia breakfast.

"What's batter bread?" asked Sarah, woken by their voices as she emerged from the alcove in the living room.

"It's what northerners call spoon bread," said Lisl, who had heard this question answered before. "It's soft inside but should have a firm, browned crust. It's yummy, especially if you mix lots of butter, some hot sauce, and your sausage with it."

"Ohmygod," said Lenore, in mock horror, "so much for my yogurt and granola breakfast regime." Sarah looked ready to eat that minute.

Meg's husband, Will, came into the kitchen in his PJs to get coffee for the two of them.

"You guys should listen to the radio," he told them. "We have ours on upstairs while we're doing our back exercises. The Gulf Coast got whammed last night and early this morning. Camille came ashore way west of where they predicted. Mississippi and Louisiana took the brunt of it. You should tune in."

Lisl switched on the TV, and they stood wordlessly in front of it, looking at the scenes of devastation. In Gulfport, there were pictures of huge oceangoing tankers gone aground. A steel barge had been picked up by the storm surge and deposited onto the highway that paralleled the beachfront, and a tugboat rested atop a collapsed house. A video camera in a helicopter flying along the ten-mile stretch of beach between Bay St. Louis and Long Beach showed that little remained of homes, businesses, roads, or trees from the beach to two blocks inland.

Because of its size and intensity, Camille had sucked up so much moisture that its storm surge had risen to an estimated height of 26 feet when it came ashore at Pass Christian, Mississippi, obliterating a three-story apartment complex along with every other structure within blocks.

Miraculously, some of those who had not evacuated had lived. There had been sustained winds of 200 miles an hour, and there were unconfirmed reports of record-low barometric pressure.

In Louisiana water had been sucked out of Lake Bourne, adding fuel to the storm surge. The surge had flooded the lowlands below New Orleans, and as the sea poured in, the great Mississippi River reversed flow. At one point the Gulf rose sixteen feet above the river.

This had all happened within the last twelve hours, and everyone, newscasters included, was struggling to make sense of it. People present who had witnessed horrific scenes would be in the middle of an interview when the realities of what they were left with would overwhelm them, and their voices would just peter out. The little group gathered by the TV in Virginia could hardly believe what they were hearing. "Oh Lord," exclaimed Lenore, "how could the sexton of that church in Pass Christian have lost his wife, ten of his eleven children and two grandchildren in a building that had survived eighteen hurricanes before Camille swept it away, leaving him with one child and one son-in-law? How would you ever get over that?" The others shook their heads in mute agreement.

The evacuations that were ordered Sunday, when it was known that they were dealing with a Category 5 hurricane, had removed 82,000 people from the area, but too many had stayed behind. Some stayed with those who could not be moved, and others stayed to take care of pets or because they had weathered so many other hurricanes in what they considered to be a hurricane-proof house. But the monstrous storm surge that came with Camille was lethal to a degree that no one from that region had ever before witnessed.

The slack-mouthed group in front of the TV was actually glad when Sam and Hans strode through the door and Sam exclaimed, "Where's breakfast?" Hans had come down to the barn to review feeding schedules he should stick to when the riders took off, and Sam was satisfied that Hans understood enough of the farm routine to get along for three days.

Turning to Elsie, Sam said, "Did you forget to ring the bell?" Everyone burst out at once, filling them in on the disaster in the Gulf. For the second time since they had gotten to the farm, Meg, who had arrived from upstairs with her coffee mug in tow, said how glad she was to be in central Virginia and not on the coast.

Sam had his mind on getting his riders off on their trip, so he flipped the TV off and moved toward the breakfast table just as Elsie was taking the high, fragile batter bread from the oven. The others followed, subdued by what they had seen but drawn to the feast in front of them. Will was the last to arrive but was the most enthusiastic eater at the table. Willa and Turtle stood at the porch door hopeful for leftovers, but were disappointed.

While they ate, Sam gave them a rundown on the trip they were about to set out on. "Today we'll ride east across the Rockfish Valley and stop at midday in Glass Hollow, which nestles up against the mountains on the northwestern side of the valley. Friends of ours have a farm there where we can tie the horses in the shade and have a leisurely picnic."

"Then we'll start up Humpback Mountain using the old Howardsville Turnpike. For the rest of the trip, we'll be in the George Washington National Forest. We have an agreement with the Forest Service to keep the turnpike open in exchange for riding over it.

"In the mid-nineteenth century the Kanawha Canal along the James River was the best means of transportation from the Piedmont section of the state to markets in the more populated Tidewater region. Farmers and merchants from the Shenandoah Valley would bring their produce over the Blue Ridge and down to the banks of the James on the turnpike. Eventually trains replaced the canals, and the train tracks also parallel the James River.

"It's not hunting season," he continued, "so we probably won't meet anyone else using the Howardsville Turnpike. You'll have to use your imaginations to people it with farmers and trades people driving ox carts, the occasional child sitting on top of the gunny sacks of corn, dogs running alongside. As you'll see, the pike maintains a very reasonable grade by traversing the entire eastern slope of Humpback Mountain. So, going up or going down, it was possible to pull heavy weights."

Suddenly he jumped to his feet and pushed his chair back from the table so forcefully that it went over backwards. "But what are we doing still talking about it?" he added. "Let's go ride it!"

SEVEN

They saddled and bridled their mounts in the barn, tucking an apple and chocolate into the big side pockets of their saddle pads. They filled canteens with water and buckled them onto the front of the saddles, where they rode flat against a horse's shoulder, easily reachable. Following Sam's instructions, they put a halter on top of the bridle, tying the lead line around each horse's neck so as to be handy when needed to tie the horse to a tree at midday. Sam also showed them how to use thongs to tie their riding raincoats to the rings on either side of the back of their saddles.

Sam, unable to stand by and watch ineptitude in any form, jerked the halter out of Stanley's hand as he stood by Packer's head, surreptitiously glancing at the others to see how they were going about it.

"Watch me, Stanley, so I don't have to show you again. You want the ring for the lead line behind his head, not on his nose. It's a tight fit with the bridle underneath it, but it'll work if you lengthen this neckpiece." Lenore and Meg, passing each other going to and from the tack room, rolled eyes at each other, and Meg said, sotto voce, "That's no way to build his confidence." "Much less his enjoyment," Lenore shot back.

Hans cornered Lisl out in the small corral checking over the loads of the pack mules, Denise and DeNephew. The mules stood, resigned and uninterested, their ears flopping, their tails swishing at the flies. Mules were designed, thought Hans idly, to make people laugh. Their tails were short and stubby, which contrasted with comic, elongated ears at their other end.

Hans put his arm around Lisl's shoulder as she checked the list in her hands. "I wish to come," he said, as he leaned over to nuzzle his face in her hair. "Everything is different here," he stated flatly, summing up her feelings so precisely that she shuddered involuntarily.

Hans took this for acknowledgement that she would miss him and turned her until she faced him, looking into her eyes for a moment. Lisl lowered her gaze. Right now she couldn't face the unspoken questions she read in the depths of his kindly brown eyes.

As if to reassure himself as well as her, he kissed her long and hard, a possessive kiss, at the same time hungrily running his hands down her body, as if to imprint its contours in his memory. Searing guilt welled up in Lisl, bringing with it a pink flush that rose up her neck and into her face. At the same time tears of confusion filled her eyes, which Hans again took for sorrow at their parting. He kissed her eyes softly, releasing her as he whispered in her ear, "You mine." Lisl fled into the barn.

Elsie, Sam, and Lisl were all riding what they called "projects," young horses being brought along slowly and getting experience with a good rider on their backs before being trusted with a guest rider.

Lisl was on a large pony named Stitch, a Connemara/thoroughbred cross that had the signature dun-colored coat with darker legs and mane. In such crosses the hope is to get in the offspring thoroughbred good looks combined with the levelheaded common sense of Connemara ponies. In Stitch's case, they had gotten just the opposite: the Connemara's heavy bone and dun color and the flighty, nervous temperament of the thoroughbred. However, Stitch was a talented jumper, and she was very useful in the barn for experienced young riders who wanted to lease her for horseshows.

As they set off, exchanging waves with the lonely figure of Hans standing outside the barn, Lisl was riding alongside Stanley to boost his confidence, hoping that Packer's plodding approach would rub off on Stitch, who was dancing sideways with excitement. They were in the middle of the line of horses. Will and Sarah followed, and finally Elsie, who, for the first part of the ride along county roads, was leading the roped-together pack mules.

Elsie was on a purebred Connemara, a small horse that had grown just a tad past the large pony size. Had he stopped growing a few inches earlier, children could have used him in large pony classes at horseshows, making him very valuable. Named Donegal, he was sturdy and deliberate, the perfect horse from which to lead line others.

Lady Mischief, with Meg on board, caught the contagious excitement from Stitch just behind her. As she pranced she swung her head up and down, jerking the reins through Meg's hands. Meg laughed, drawing them up again as she attempted to settle Lady Mischief into line.

From Will came the old family joke, "That horse needs a stage...there's one leaving in ten minutes!" Everyone laughed, caught up in the high spirits of a trip so long anticipated and finally underway.

Lenore, on Challenger, was just ahead of Meg and behind Sam, who was riding a young, big-boned Canadian warm blood that had grown to seventeen hands, tall for a horse. He had been born on the farm, and Sam had named him for his favorite bourbon, Rebel Yell, but called him Rebel for short. He would eventually grow into his height and fill out, but at the moment he had a slightly awkward look, his bone structure disproportionate to his skinny frame.

The farm lane turned onto a gravel road that allowed

them to ride two by two, undisturbed except for the occasional hay wagon or piece of farm machinery rumbling by. They learned quickly how to fall back into a single line while these passed, and then regroup as they had been before.

Rebel, unused to leading, was urged on by Sam, who tickled him with his crop and applied heel pressure to the barrel of the horse. As the little caravan moved west across the valley floor, Lenore rode alongside him, giving Challenger small checks with the reins to make sure he didn't overtake Rebel.

"Lenore," asked Sam, "I saw from the information sheet that you and Stanley have two children. Why didn't you bring them on the ride?"

"I don't usually take them when I'm on assignment," she answered, "but I have to admit I was tempted this time."

Some of the liveliness went out of her face as she continued. "Our daughter is twelve and would have enjoyed it, but our ten-year-old son is autistic. He isn't up to it, and when we go anywhere, a friend comes to stay at our house. The secret to keeping Roddy happy is to keep things as routine as possible.

"Taking Claire out of the picture upsets him badly, especially when we're gone too. It's hard on Claire; she's become a sort of hostage to her brother. Luckily for us she is mature for her age, and understands on some level."

Lenore wanted to turn the tables, so she inquired, "How about you? How did you and Elsie get into this business? Has this always been a horse farm?"

"No," he answered. "My grandparents bought it right after World War II. The seller was a widow who had lost her husband in the war and was moving into Waynesboro. She thought she was selling a rundown house and overused fields. What Granddad Crawford could see was all the timber on the slopes of Long Arm Mountain."

As he spoke he gestured behind him in the direction from which they had just come. "In those days mountain land was

considered nearly useless, but he figured the postwar building boom would create a high demand for timber. He knew
he could teach his pair of Suffolk Punch draft horses to log
the slopes of the mountain and go places where no machine
would go. Granddad also liked the fact that the creek ran
through the property. He could raise cows without worrying
about their water supply most years.

"My dad really loved the horse logging—loved the way it
left almost no imprint on the land compared to big machines,
and he had the patience to put in endless training time with
his horses. I had helped him enough with his horse logging
operation to know I didn't want to make a living that way. Besides, by the time Dad died he had taken most of the valuable
timber. There'll be another crop in thirty years or so, but you
gotta be patient.

"I worked my way through Virginia Tech and majored
in mechanical engineering so I would have some choices, but
timing is everything. Dad died right before I graduated, and
the kaleidoscope shifted just enough so that choices were never made. Suddenly I went from unentangled to so entangled
that I couldn't see my way out of it."

Then, as if he realized he'd gone too far and sounded
whiny, he added, "But I do love what I do. Showing people
this beautiful part of the world is fun."

Lisl pondered, silently, at his use of the pronoun "I." It
was as if Elsie didn't exist and wasn't five horses behind them
handling the two pack mules on her own. Not to mention
the crucial role that Lisl herself played in his operation. Lenore's anger flared, but just as she was about to speak up they
came upon the state highway that bisected the valley running
north to south. Sam motioned for the group to tighten up so
they could all cross together.

"Elsie," ordered Sam, "Get those good for nothin' mules
up here NOW!" Neither Elsie's expression nor her actions
gave any indication that she had heard him, although she
couldn't have failed to do so. Lenore reacted instantly.

"DON'T YELL AT HER! She's the one doing the hard work here."

Sam turned in his saddle, his face giving away the anger he felt. He was about to yell at Lenore, too, but quickly thought better of it. Without replying, he concentrated instead on checking for the perfect moment to cross Route 151. When nothing was coming from either direction, he escorted his caravan safely across the highway.

They were again on a county road and fell into single file until they turned onto a dirt road that took off in the direction of Humpback Mountain. Its bulk and height, and the way it dominated the western end of the valley, gave it an importance that none of the other mountains around it possessed.

The hump for which the mountain had been named was at the top, but looping, progressively smaller repetitions of it rolled off into the valley, curving north, and making the mountain part of the valley, not just its western border.

Sam knew they were freed from worry about traffic, so he suggested they have a short trot. "Don't worry, Stanley," Sam said, "we put you in that western saddle so all you have to do is sit there and hold on to the pommel. Your horse has the smoothest trot of all; you'll never know you're moving faster."

Stanley looked dubious, but when Packer shuffled off after the others, he found that Sam was right. A big grin spread over his face as he drew up beside the others. Lenore was happy to see his pleasure and rode beside him the short distance to the Henderson's farm at the foot of Humpback, where they were to eat lunch.

The farm stood on the last open, flat, fertile ground before the forested slopes of the mountain rose up from it. As they tied their horses to saplings along the creek bottom, Bob Henderson showed the riders patches of ginger growing wild in the woods. Right now its leaves looked like all the leaves around it, but later in the fall it would turn a telltale burnished orange, and Bob would spend hours roaming the coves of the mountain, harvesting the root and replanting as he went along.

Bob bent his tall frame over and pulled up a ginseng plant to show them the root. "This here," he said, "doesn't look like much, but in a good year I can make $20,000 or so selling ginseng on the export market. It goes into health and nutrition supplements, and those Korean men must think it helps them with the ladies 'cause they buy lots of it!"

Bob's mother, Jane, had set out their first meal of the trip on the picnic table in the yard. The fragrance of her home-made bread drew the riders immediately, and soon they were making inroads on the mound of potato salad with bacon and onions and the thinly-sliced Virginia ham.

"Don't eat too much ham," warned Sam, "or you'll be thirsty all afternoon." Fred Henderson, Jane's husband, came out of the house with a plate of cheddar and goat cheese, nibbling as he came.

"The Mennonites in the Shenandoah Valley make these," he said, addressing everyone, "and you can take it from me they are good!" To prove his point, he popped a piece of cheese in his mouth as he set the plate on the table.

While they ate, they listened to Fred explain how their part of Nelson County, Glass Hollow, had gotten its name.

"No," he said, "glass has never been blown here, but used to be that the Glass family lived around these parts." Will, unnoticed, had snuck off and was napping flat on his back in shade thrown by the large leaves of a young Paulownia tree. He had put his neck scarf over his face, and it rose and fell slightly as he slept.

When Sam rousted them for the afternoon ride, they re-luctantly said goodbye to the Hendersons, remounted, and left the open fields and domestic peace of Glass Hollow. The transition was abrupt, for as soon as they began climbing the eastern slope of Humpback Mountain, they were riding in jungle-like growth. The canopy of oaks, tulip poplars, and beech trees towered above them, while in some places the late-summer weeds encroached on their trail.

Wild grapevine the size of a human fist held some trees prisoner, growing up from the ground and sucking the life out of trees over the course of years. The eye could follow the line of the vine upward and see where it looped between trees in search of more victims. Squirrels used these swinging bridges as shortcuts from tree to tree in midair. The three innocent-looking leaves of poison oak stuck out toward the riders at eye level on furry vines that encircled the lower parts of tree trunks.

Moisture hung in the air and the ground underfoot was soft from all the rain. Initially the trail followed Mill Creek up the side of the mountain. It ran swift and bloated, with eroded sides concave under the lip of banks on either side showing where the reddish clay had given way and washed into the valley.

The group was as silent as they had been loquacious at lunch, watching where their horses put down their hooves, and keeping an eye out for the occasional branch reaching out to scratch them from a blackberry bush or a wild rose. The forest seemed to be alive and actively growing as they moved through it; its life force, if not malevolent, showing itself at the very least defensive against intruders.

Sam cursed himself for not taking the time to come through here with his weed-eater the week before. He had forgotten how quickly the forest could take back a trail in the semi-tropical climate of Virginia.

EIGHT

By four o'clock they had reached the Howardsville Turnpike and left the steep path along Mill Creek for the wider, better-graded nineteenth-century route over the Blue Ridge. At first it was hard to realize that this had been a major thoroughfare in the early years of the Virginia Colony, but then they came to a short, handsomely constructed bridge that took the turnpike over a small ravine with a creek running down it.

The bridge was below the level of the turnpike, but in approaching it you could see the brick arches that supported the road over the ravine. The care with which the archway had been constructed gave a clue as to the weight of vehicles that once crossed it, and it became easier to imagine the roadway choked with animals going to market, the air filled with the cries of their owners urging them along.

They were riding through a grove of mature white oak trees, their branches creating a canopy so thick that shade from them had cut off all competing vegetation. Twisting in his saddle, Sam spoke loud enough so that all of them could hear him.

"See these white oaks? Now they are kings of the forest, but when this turnpike was in use the king of that era was the American chestnut. In those days one out of every four trees would have been a chestnut, some of them over one hundred feet tall. Old men have told me that there were so many of them that in early summer their creamy blooms turned the sides of the mountains white, as if it had been snowing."

"But then the blight got them, right?" queried Meg. "Where did it come from?"

"Sometime in the early years of the twentieth century it came into this country from Asia," replied Sam, "some say from Japan, on a tree sent to the Bronx Zoo. In any case it spread like wildfire. The chestnut was always prized for lumber, but it wasn't only that industry that suffered when the trees began to die. Farmers gathered its nuts in the fall and used them all winter to fatten their hogs. The tanning industry extracted tannic acid from chestnut bark, which was used as a dye in shoe making. The chestnut blight was a major reason for the decline of agriculture and industry in rural areas."

Sarah chimed in. "When I was stationed in Washington, we were asked to speed up the importation of Chinese chestnut trees into this country so they could backcross resistance into American chestnuts. I hope it works."

Toward the end of the afternoon, they fell into an agreeable silence, lulled by the humid air and the methodical steps of the horses climbing upward. Sarah, looking down, marveled at the sure way that Sassafras put her feet down, avoiding stones, and on the downhill side giving a wide berth to rough spots that had eroded away.

Elsie, freed from leading the mules who had been turned loose to plod along in front of her, found herself thinking of the incident that morning when Sam had yelled at her. Why did he insist on humiliating her? She tried to think when it had begun, but couldn't put her finger on a certain time. Had she brought a certain frustration with her when she married? Certainly her upbringing had given her equestrian ambitions far removed from the work she had done with horses since she married.

She had no memory of her father, who had died in a car accident when she was just eighteen months old. Joseph

Sanders was a superb horseman who had made sure that his baby girl was comfortable around ponies before she was even able to walk.

After his death, Eleanor, his beautiful, flighty, nonathletic wife, floundered in widowhood and could not cope with what she saw as her new diminished self. She began to think of Elsie as a weight that kept her from a social life, rather than as the apple of her eye. Eleanor had never been enthusiastic about the idea of children; it was Joseph who wanted them—and now he was gone.

Luckily for Eleanor, not many months went by before she caught the eye of John Greenfield, a commercial real estate investor who had done very well for himself in New York City. A recent divorcee, he lived in a large house on the water in the Connecticut suburbs.

John attended the local Presbyterian Church, and one day after the service he spied a tall, willowy woman with her back to him, leaning in toward the person she was talking to in animated conversation, blonde wisps of hair floating around her head in the slight breeze. He found an excuse to meet her, and soon he was squiring Eleanor around. Before a year was up, John and Eleanor were married, and Elsie and Eleanor moved into "Seagate."

John was never mean to Elsie, and he was generous in providing for her every need, but she was not his child, and her existence threatened the life he most aspired to—the parties, charity balls, travel and New York theater that Eleanor also loved.

Elsie couldn't remember a time when she hadn't felt like an appendage in that household. She was well looked after, not so much by her mother, but by a revolving set of nannies, maids and babysitters that had taken Eleanor's place.

From age six, when she got her first pony, she knew where she stood. If she stayed in the background, John would buy her anything she wanted, and what she wanted as she got older was to ride competitively. A small stable and a riding ring were built on the property, and Captain Schmidt, an Austrian rider of the old school, was her coach.

His was a difficult personality—not lavish with praise—but he took pride in making an extraordinary rider out of Elsie, and found her as gritty and courageous as any of the Austrian Military Academy cadets that he had instructed early in his career.

On weekends, when her mother and stepfather were often entertaining on his yacht, Elsie and the Captain would be at horseshows. After she had done the rounds of the little local shows in the early years, they took the plunge into the "A" level shows; the $10,000 ponies eventually replaced by a $50,000 show horse that she named "Eisle," her name spelled backwards.

Even John and Eleanor came to watch and took notice when Elsie won the medal for the best junior rider in the country, performing in Madison Square Garden. When the announcement was made, Captain Schmidt, who had been standing alongside Elsie near the ingate, burst into tears, much to his embarrassment.

After this achievement, Elsie set her sights on making the American Olympic Equestrian Team, deciding to go all out for this rather than going to college.

In the early fall of Elsie's senior year in high school, the bottom fell out again for her and her mother when John was struck by an aneurism. He was rushed to the hospital but died six hours later. At first it looked as if he had left them well off, but then they discovered that John had many debts going back years that had left big holes in his estate.

"Seagate" and its furnishings were sold, along with the horses, and Eleanor was left with barely enough money to refurbish a small house she had inherited from her aunt in The Plains, Virginia. Elsie, forced to rethink her future, knew she needed a college education and decided on Virginia Tech. It had a veterinary school if she ended up going that route, and so she applied for and received a scholarship.

Elsie had always been a high-achieving student, as riding and studying had taken up all the time she had for as long as she could remember. But the life she led didn't produce any close friendships. While she counted as friends some of her fellow competitors on the show circuit, she had not been home for most of the sleepovers and birthday parties that form the basis of lifelong friendships.

Predictably, her mother fell apart at the seams again. Elsie, now an adult, took charge, seemingly unsurprised by their newest change in circumstance. What she missed, even more than the horses and her life on the show circuit, was the gruff affection that had grown up between her and Captain Schmidt, forged over countless weekdays of lessons and weekends spent campaigning.

They had made do when rain turned an arena into a mud pit, or when a horse at the peak of its training came up lame on the day of the show. Of course they had also shared the successes, but what Captain Schmidt most admired about Elsie was her imperturbability.

Unlike most of the females he knew, she didn't react emotionally; she didn't cry when she had been dumped unceremoniously by her pony at the base of a jump, or wasn't in the ribbons in a class in which she thought she had done well. She had not even cried when her first pony, Foxy Loxie, developed an inoperable twisted gut and had to be put down. Neither had she left the stable when the vet administered the lethal dose. She had stayed with the pony, cradling its head in her lap.

Perhaps, Captain Schmidt had thought, she had put up her emotional barriers early in life, locking out the vulnerability to being crushed by what life brings. In any case, he recognized in her the same potential that he had seen twenty years before in the best of his Austrian recruits.

By the time that Elsie met Sam, she was using her considerable talent with horses to be able to ride without the expense of owning a horse, her Olympic dreams pushed way to the back of her mind. When Sam came to know her story, he was amazed that she had no self-pity; what she recounted to him was just the way it was, nothing more. Even Elsie may not have recognized the lingering resilience of that Olympic hope.

About 6 p.m. they reached a large, open oval, about half the length of a football field. A few old apple trees were clues that this had once been a homestead, although there was nothing else to indicate it. A small stream, which started at a spring coming from a jumble of rocks near the woods, cut off the western third of the clearing. The horses were tethered for the night in the good grass it offered, while the riders laid claim to the rest of the clearing.

Another distinguishing feature of the open land was the low bulk of an ancient Indian midden near the trees on the downhill slant of the oval. The group took advantage of the flattest land, between the midden and the woods on the uphill side, which had occasional clumps of mountain laurel and rhododendron offering some privacy. They went about setting up their tents and spreading their sleeping bags.

"Lisl!" called Meg, as she and Will argued about what to attach to the stakes they had put in the ground. "Our tent is listing, what did we do wrong?" Lisl hurried over, laughing as she saw that their tent would not make it through the night— even a windless night.

"Here, let me help you," she said, collapsing what they had done so far and showing them how to start again.

Meanwhile Sam had an open fire going, while Elsie unpacked the Dutch oven and her kitchen utensils and began preparing supper. Sarah, who was helping, had drawn water from the spring. As Elsie passed the water bucket, Sarah dropped in purification tablets and leaned over to pick up the lid for the oven.

Lenore and Stanley had put their tent up in the woods and were sitting outside it, resting and watching the activity in the clearing. As Lenore idly rubbed her bootless feet, Stanley leaned closer to her and, in a low voice, asked, "When do you think was the last time Elsie and Sam had a conversation?"

"I dunno," she pondered, "maybe before they were married!?"

Just then Sarah walked nearby on the way to her tent. "You guys in the woods are going to be in the dark soon. We've still got some daylight, but now that we're getting on in August, the days are shorter. You really notice it in the evening."

Stanley nodded in agreement and added, "Even though I haven't been a student for two decades, August still makes me feel sad that summer is about to end, and anxious about school beginning."

Their supper that first night was sumptuous. Since there was only one fire and two dishes to cook, Elsie baked her blackberry buckle first, using berries she had picked and frozen when they came into season a month before. When it was done she moved it to the outskirts of the fire and built a little pile of embers around it to keep it warm.

Sam put the big frying pan on the fire and let the heat radiating from it move the air above it before throwing on a hunk of butter. Before it could brown he snuggled the trout together in the pan, slipping fronds of dill from Elsie's herb garden inside the cavity of each fish, and salting and peppering the fish.

By this time everyone had gathered and was watching intently as dinner slowly took shape. Sarah had made the salad, while a loaf of Elsie's homemade bread completed the meal. Dark fell as they devoured the blackberry cobbler, and when it was over it seemed too early to turn in.

"Let's play charades," cried Meg. "It's particularly fun when people don't know each other very well."

"Count me out," responded Will good-humoredly. "I'm going to get in my sleeping bag and read."

"Sure," countered Meg, "how are you going to see?" Magician-like, Will drew a miner's headlamp from his pocket, put it around his forehead and turned it on.

"See!" he said triumphantly as he moved off, "L.L. Bean supplies all needs!"

Neither this defection nor the next surprised Meg. "I'd better not play either," mumbled Elsie, looking down. "I need to organize for tomorrow." The third person to speak up did surprise her.

Lisl rose and said, "I'm tired and I think I'll turn in." The women objected, but she was adamant and said goodnight. That left Lenore, Meg, Sarah, Stanley and Sam, and they agreed to play the men against the women.

The women were initially easy on the men. They gave them assignments to act out *Madame Butterfly* and *The Sun Also Rises*, whereas the men had taken a tougher tack.

Stanley had had an argument, a few weeks past, with a business friend whose parting shot was to refer him to Adam Smith's *The Wealth of Nations*. Stung, he had taken it from the library and had been arrested by the fact that it's entire title was *An Enquiry into the Nature and the Causes of the Wealth of Nations*. Knowing this would cause a furor, he wrote it on a piece of paper and threw it into the pot.

Sam, tired after a long ride and a good supper, came up with *Thus Spake Zarathustra*, having no idea whether it was a book, a quotation from the Bible, or a song. He just remembered hearing it and thought it would be difficult, so in it went. For good measure, he threw in *Ulysses*, as well, which he had managed to avoid reading in high school and college.

The women got madder and madder at the men, as the time it took for the women to act out their assignments got longer and the men's times got shorter. The men found this hilarious.

"You can't expect us to know full titles; even college professors refer to it as *The Wealth of Nations*!" fumed Meg, tossing her hair and adding dismissively, "whomever put *Ulysses* in spelled it wrong!"

"That's the ancient Greek spelling," Stanley shot back, and both men bent double laughing.

Lenore, Sarah and Meg wised up in the next round, and soon Sam found himself having to act out *Ben-Hur.* He groaned when he opened the piece of paper and managed to read it. The women gave him extra time to think, and finally he indicated he was ready.

Sam was certain he would tip off his partner's mind with Big Ben, as he tried to make himself into a clock face with his arms pointing at the time it was at that moment. "Clock" Stanley got, but not Big Ben, so then Sam went off in an entirely different direction, building an imaginary tower from the ground up, as in the tower of the Houses of Parliament that is home to Big Ben.

Since he was standing between the fire and his audience, his efforts were backlit and magnified by the fire. He was outlined for his viewers, but they could not see his face, which registered his annoyance.

When they began laughing at his frantic attempt to mime building a tower, he abruptly switched his method again. Stopping mid-gesture, he started to pull on his right ear. Instantly Stanley perked up and said, "sounds like." Sam nodded in assent, and then a low growl of "ggrrrrr" came from his throat.

"BURR!" yelled Stanley, followed in quick succession by "KERR" and "FUR!"

"NO NO NO NO NO!!!!!" ranted Sam, unable to mask his frustration. "I can't play this anymore. Stanley, you just don't GET it, do you? What a stupid game," he muttered as he walked away from the fireside.

In seconds Meg rose from the ground and, challenging his departing back, said, "Why is it that you have such a strong need to dump on others? The whole POINT of charades is to have fun making a fool of yourself. Only a self-centered jerk could get so pissed off over a game!"

Sam spun on his heel, furious now, but in the process

of turning got control of himself. In a calmer voice he said to them all, "If you sleep lightly and hear someone moving around in the middle of the night, don't worry, it's just me, checking on the horses. I'm going to sleep down there near them. Please see the fire is out before you turn in." Then he turned and walked away.

Meg and Lenore exchanged looks and rose to their feet. "Well, I guess that's the end of charades for the night," joked Stanley, as he and the others rose stiffly from their cross-legged positions around the fire. "See you all in the morning." Everyone helped to put out what remained of the fire, and then they disappeared into the shadows toward their tents.

Lisl lay rigid on top of her sleeping bag in the moist air. She had overheard Sam's outburst, and she had also heard his statement about checking on the horses in the middle of the night. She was desperate to talk to him; she knew that their situation had blinded his judgment, and that he, like she, was becoming obsessed with their predicament. But here he was, jeopardizing his best chance for a major boost for his business that would come from a favorable article by Lenore.

"I need to get to him," she said quietly to herself. "We've got two more days on this ride and he can make it up, but only if he starts out tomorrow morning with a totally different attitude."

Lisl knew it would be several hours before she could go to him, and hoped that if she failed to hear his footsteps she would hear the horses stir while he was checking on them. She lay there, sometimes lightly dreaming, sometimes near consciousness, willing herself not to think about Sam and failing utterly.

Even half-asleep she felt his physical presence so strongly that she was embarrassed at her response. Turning to lie on her stomach with her head on her arms she tried to quell the passion that she felt.

Lying like this, she heard low nickering among the horses. "I shouldn't go to him like this," she thought, even as she rose and knelt on one knee by the entrance to the tent, listening for sounds around her. There were none, except for gentle snores that rose unevenly from the Lapsleys' tent.

The risk she was taking had the perverse effect of encouraging her. "This is a new Lisl," she thought to herself as she rose, moving noiselessly through the trees as she circled round until she could hear, and then see, the small stream. The waning moon had just set, and after she jumped the creek she paused a moment to let her eyes adjust.

Slowly the dark bulks of the horses took shape, and after a minute she could make out Sam's bent figure, leaning over to check Geronimo's hobble. She didn't want to startle either Geronimo or Sam, so she walked directly towards them, whispering Sam's name as she approached.

He had on shorts, no shirt, and his riding boots. He loomed large in the dark as he separated from the horses and in one movement scooped her off her feet and carried her to the stream and across it in one big step, aiming to put the psychological if not physical protection of the Indian midden between them and the sleeping guests.

"Sam, you mustn't lose it again on this ride or you will - - - " she whispered urgently, until his lips silenced her.

"I know, I know," he countered. "I promise it won't happen again." Slowly he set her down, and then turned her around to untie the bow of her sleeping shift at the back of the neck. As it slipped to the ground, he reached over her shoulders with both arms and folded them along her breast bone, gently laying his head down on hers Surprised and aroused, she sucked in air sharply.

Anticipating this, Sam's hand moved upward to cup her mouth and cut off sound, still holding her a willing prisoner as he palmed her core backwards against his.

Suddenly, over the heat of her body, a thought forced its way into her mind. If I died this instant, she thought, I would die knowing what ecstasy is. As he gently released her from his grasp, she slipped, rag doll-like, unable to stand, down onto the slight incline at her feet. Sam made a bed of her shift, folding his shorts for her pillow. He sat on the ground beside her, his hands trembling as he wrestled off his western riding boots.

When he lay down and rolled onto his side, he was hypnotized by how small and white her body was next to his large, suntanned frame. Supporting himself on his elbow, he traced her eyebrows, the hairline that framed her face, her earlobes, nose and collarbones, his finger moving deliberately and softly, in a caress. If she had been a newborn, the gesture couldn't have been gentler.

Then, kneeling, he ran his fingers through her hair and cupped her head in both his hands. Slowly he lifted her head a little off the ground and leaning down, gave her eyelids chaste kisses before arousing her with a questioning kiss on the lips.

As she rolled towards him with her arms extended, she answered wordlessly, letting the sound of the water running downhill through a small rock garden drown out all caution and consciousness.

Elsie, retiring early, had been asleep since her head hit the balled up sweatshirt serving as a pillow. She had decided not to pitch a tent, since Sam was sleeping with the horses and since it didn't look like rain—for once. She had dragged her sleeping bag past the edge of the bushes and bedded down where she had an unimpeded view of the sky.

Elsie was able to count one falling star before succumbing to sleep. When she woke there was quiet all around her, and she wondered what time it was. She turned onto her stomach and reached for her watch and the little battery flashlight, which were lying inside her hat just in front of the bedroll. As she was in the process of withdrawing them from the hat, something distracted her eye. She glanced up, and saw a slight silhouette slip from the open pasture onto the path through the bushes where the tents were.

Looks like Lisl, she thought, coming back from a trip to the loo. Then she froze with the realization that the one-hole outhouse was in the opposite direction. The watch and flashlight dropped back into the hat, and tears sprang into Elsie's eyes as she collapsed from her elbows, hid her head in the sweatshirt and beat her fists on the ground.

NINE

THE NEXT MORNING, SITTING WITH THE others around the campfire eating Elsie's Canadian bacon and egg sandwiches for breakfast, Lisl was horrified at the proximity of the Indian midden to where they all were gathered. That kind of recklessness has got to stop, she thought to herself, and knew, sitting there, that it would be she who would have to enforce it.

When Lenore and Stanley joined the circle around the fire, Sam got up and went over to make his apology directly to Stanley.

"I'm sorry for my behavior last night, Stanley. I was tired and probably should have just begged off. In any case I apologize for my rude behavior."

"Apology accepted," responded Stanley, looking at Sam with a smile. "Luckily I'm better with numbers than with words."

"So, Sam," said Lenore, "tell us where we're going today."

"We've got a good long ride ahead of us," answered Sam, "but it's beautiful territory, and you'll begin to get occasional vistas of the Shenandoah Valley and the Allegheny Mountains to the west, as well as the Rockfish Valley. We will be traveling south on trails that stay just below the ridge. Our destination is an old abandoned church, from the days before the Blue Ridge Parkway when these hollows had people living in them and they used the mountain tops for summer grazing. It's only about seven miles south of here, but it's slow going."

"Oh, it sounds beautiful," exclaimed Sarah.

"It is," said Sam, "but there is one section of the trail that is pretty steep and rocky. When we get there early this afternoon, I'll ask you all to get off your horses and lead them down that part. It's only about half a mile long."

When he noticed Sarah's worried expression Sam added, "Don't worry, the horses won't overtake you. They are trained to stay at the end of the length of your reins." This didn't completely restore Sarah's confidence, but just then Sam suggested that they get their horses ready to move off.

As they were doing so, a man entered the clearing stooped under a load of two-by-fours that stuck out of the top of his backpack and slanted forward over his head. He had on the uniform of a forest ranger, and when he came up to their campsite Sam greeted him.

"Here I am, trying to give these guests the impression that they are miles from nowhere, and here you come from civilization, McCray," he said in a joking voice.

"Sorry to disappoint you," responded the ranger. "I'm on my way into the ranger cabin a mile from here to install some shelves. We've got a young man coming in to live for a month while he does a forest survey."

"Well, he'll need those shelves then," said Sam, and offered him the last of the coffee.

"No thanks," said McCray. "It'll be a long day, but I'm hoping to finish the job today and get back home tonight, so I'd best keep moving."

"Makes sense to me," said Sam. "Before you go, what do you know about the weather?" McCray took off his cap and scratched his head.

"Seems like to me I heard the radio say we might get some rain—a backlash from that hurricane that now they're callin' a tropical storm—but to tell you the truth I wasn't listening too carefully, it don't pay to. The weatherman proposes but the Lord disposes," he said as he settled his cap back on his head.

"We can deal with rain," commented Sam, "especially since we will have a roof over our heads tonight. Good luck to you."

"Same to y'all," echoed the departing ranger, making his way out of the clearing.

His leave-taking was a signal that it was time for them to move off, and Lisl was agreeably surprised to find that a routine had been established. They were able to pack and saddle up in just over a half-hour. When they left, the only traces of their overnight stay were a few meadow muffins where the horses had been hobbled.

The morning was serene. There was no wind, and the hazy atmosphere turned their occasional sights into the valley into shimmering, indistinct vistas. There was nothing ugly to be seen, looking either east or west, and the forest through which they rode was a deep green.

Occasionally the mountain laurel and the understory of small trees would open up to the west and give them views into the broad expanse of the Shenandoah Valley sweeping down from northeast to southwest. The South Fork of the Shenandoah River was a lazy line of connected "S" curves as it made its way slowly north toward the Potomac River.

Within the curves, cows grazed on the bounty of the alluvial soil that had built up over the centuries. Occasional silos punctured the sky, and farmhouses shimmered in the build-up of heat, the umbrellas of old oaks and maples around them offering some relief. There were a few remaining stands of forest in the valley, but by and large it was taken over by good-sized farms.

The Allegheny Mountains formed the western boundary of the valley, higher and more arresting than the Blue Ridge range where the riders were. The thought crossed Lenore's mind that should anything go wrong, she could easily walk off the mountain she was riding over, whereas the taller of the distant Alleghenies looked wilder and more difficult to maneuver through.

When they sometimes glimpsed the Rockfish Valley to their east, the contrast was striking. There was much more forestland, and even the valley itself was undulated with hills. The valley had an intimate scale to it, giving their bird's eye view the feeling of peeping through a keyhole.

Below them, in the middle of a field, there was the miniature figure of a farmer on a tractor. He made his way between rows of corn, disappearing among the furrows and then reappearing at the end of the row to make a U turn. Occasionally horses shared a field with cows. There were still some farmers who used horsepower to cultivate their farms.

Two hours after they had set off, they stopped for a picnic lunch at a large rock outcropping facing west. Behind it was fairly dense vegetation, so it took a while for everyone to untie their lead lines from around their waists and find a tree with a notch low enough to use to tie their horses. Elsie used the time to make sandwiches and unpack a bag of fruit. Lisl volunteered to stay near the horses, while the others made their way out to admire the view from the rock.

Lenore came up behind Stanley and threw her arms around his waist. "How are you and Packer getting along?" she inquired, her chin resting on his shoulder.

"I think he has accepted the fact that I know nothing about riding, and therefore has put himself in charge of me, which suits me fine," responded Stanley. Lenore gave him a big squeeze.

"You talk poor," she said. "I think you two make a pretty dashing pair."

"Looks can deceive," he answered ruefully, although he was pleased by her compliment.

As Sarah came out onto the rock formation and looked south, she marveled at how the Blue Ridge widened out between the Rockfish and the Shenandoah valleys. Where they were, Humpback Mountain was all that separated the two, but a few miles south there were several mountains and an upland plateau that stretched far to the southwest before descending to the Shenandoah Valley.

"That's where we're heading," said Sam, stopping near her. "The church we're staying in tonight is on the first part of that plateau." Then, waving his arm to the north, encompassing with one sweep the flat, fertile land in the Shenandoah Valley, he added, "You're looking at the breadbasket of the Confederacy. That's why there were so many battles fought right in this area, because the crops went downstate via trains that went through the Crozet Tunnel at Rockfish Gap.

"Crozet had been an engineer for Napoleon's armies before he moved to the United States to teach engineering at West Point. Later he helped found Virginia Military Institute. He oversaw public works for the state of Virginia and engineered this tunnel. At the time it was opened in 1858, it was the longest tunnel in the United States, at just under a mile. It was built with black powder explosives and the hand labor of Irish immigrants and slaves. It was difficult and dangerous work; many died from diseases that tore through the work camps, or from explosive accidents."

Stanley, sitting with his feet dangling into thin air and already munching his sandwich, said, "At one point I was addicted to Civil War literature. I remember there were parts of the Shenandoah Valley that changed hands between the Yankees and the Southern forces every few months during the war. No matter which side controlled the area, they made constant demands on the farmers, requisitioning crops and stealing livestock. Farmers went to great lengths to hide their horses, but that's difficult to do. It must have been so hard on the civilian population." From where they sat, it didn't take a large leap of the imagination to see raiding parties moving up and down the valley.

Sam didn't leave them long for their imaginings, however. After giving them time to finish their picnic and catch a short siesta, he told them, "This next part of the trail is what I was describing to you at breakfast. Lead your horse and stay the length of the lead line ahead. You will be just fine if you watch where you put your feet and don't keep looking back at your horse. The horses will take care of themselves. As I said, they stop when you stop. We haven't had an accident since we started these rides, and we don't want to ruin that record."

When they reluctantly moved off the rock outcropping and went to get their horses, they found that Lisl had already untied them and was holding their lead lines. In short order they were underway, Sam leading, Elsie in the middle of the pack this time, and Lisl bringing up the rear with the pack-horses loose in front of her.

The downward slope was not terribly steep, but the going was slow and sloppy in soil loosened by frequent rains. Meg, used to leading horses, noticed Sarah, ahead of her, unable to stop looking around to make sure that Sassafras was not about to run her down. She started to say something reassuring to her, but realized Sam might hear her and scold Sarah, which would only make the problem worse, so she kept her mouth shut.

She did wonder why, instead of going straight down the worst of the incline, the trail makers hadn't put in a series of switchbacks, which would be easier on horses and humans. Everyone was quiet as, heads down, they picked their way along.

There was dense forest on either side of them, which lent a claustrophobic feeling to their surroundings. Erosion had taken its toll, and at one point horses and people had worn a deep trench between the sides of the trail, which were at eye level for those in the trench.

Meg, to vary the routine and to stay out of the mud, on impulse scrambled up the bank on the right side and began walking along, leading Lady Mischief from above. Pleased with her discovery, she called to the others from above, "It's less muddy up here."

Just then she felt her right foot catch in something. Expecting it to give, she leaned forward. But it was a root, attached at both ends, and it held its captive, even as the rest of her body moved forward. Surprised and off-balance, Meg heard a twig snap, and only as pain ripped up her leg and her foot worked its way free did she realize the twig was a bone in her leg. Just as this realization was dawning on her, the momentum of her forward movement sent her pitching headfirst down the embankment, landing just in front of a startled Lady Mischief.

As though from another planet, Meg heard Will's worried voice calling, "Meg, are you all right?" Meg found she was able to sit up and, strangely, was able to view the situation with a curious objectivity, as if she were commenting on the state of someone else who had been in an accident. She looked down at her right leg. The broken bone had moved very close to the surface of the skin, although it hadn't broken through. "No," she replied in a matter-of-fact voice, "I broke my leg."

In an anguished voice Will cried "NOOOO!" which brought the caravan to an abrupt stop. Lenore, who had turned to see if she could help, caught Geronimo's lead line as Will ran to Meg's side and kneeled beside her. He enfolded her shoulders in his hands as he looked down where she was looking, at the base of her right leg. Against the pale skin of her leg, just above the ankle, the bottom part of the fibula was pressing against skin. He felt the acid rush of his lunch rising into his throat but fought it down, squeezing her shoulders together as if the force of that movement might cancel the pain he knew she was feeling. "Oh God, Mama, what have you done?" came out from between his gritted teeth.

By this time Sam had made his way back to where Meg sat. He looked pale with worry, thought Meg, not a good sign given their distance from help. Will rose to his feet as Sam approached. "She's got a break for sure," announced Will.

"What have you got for pain killers and for splinting it?" At this Sam's white face went whiter.

"I have Aspirin," he began, but was interrupted by Will's roar.

"ASPIRIN!" Will spat out. "What about codeine, or something that might actually help the pain?" Will didn't actually look at Sam, as he was afraid he might hit him if he did. With effort he controlled himself and said, "Well, what about a splint?"

Lisl, who came up at just that moment, said, "I'll find a stick we can use for a splint and make some strips out of my extra shirt." At this Will let out a groan, as it dawned on him how ill prepared they were to deal with a serious accident.

Elsie didn't approach, but stood passively by Donegal, holding onto his halter as if he might escape at any moment. Lenore, struck by the look of fear in Elsie's face, dismounted from Challenger and put an arm around her shoulders. "Elsie," she said kindly, "may I hold Donegal for you so you can help?" As if paralyzed, Elsie clung to Donegal's halter, wordless.

Unable to hide her annoyance, Lenore shoved Challenger's lead line into Elsie's hands and caught up with Lisl, who had climbed the bank to find a branch to serve as a splint. "Jesus," began Lenore, "now what do we do?"

"We will have to get her out of here as fast as possible," answered Lisl. "That break could come through the skin any time, and from then it's just a matter of time until infection sets in."

"Where's the closest hospital," asked Lenore.

"Waynesboro," responded Lisl. "That's the easy part. The hard part is getting her out of here. Meg will have to ride out." Both women grimaced at the thought.

"Here, this will do," said Lisl, as she broke a small branch off of a sapling and stripped it of leaves. They returned to the caravan lined up in the muddy gully that was the trail.

Stanley had moved in to stand behind Meg as she sat, so that she could lean against his legs. Will had straightened out both her legs, and he had raised her enough so that her chaps could be removed and the blue jeans on her right leg rolled up. As Lisl came up with the splint, Sam took it and said, "Tell Elsie to come here—she's had some first aid training."

Lenore, overhearing this, said "Sam, you'd better go talk to her; she's in no condition to help anyone." Sam swore under his breath as he handed the splint back to Lisl and went to find Elsie.

Lisl knelt down by Meg and, smiling at her, said, "Sam should never have bragged about not ever having an accident on these rides. I think the devil heard him!"

"No doubt," answered Meg, holding her leg beneath the knee so that Will and Lisl could splint it.

"How's the pain?" asked Lisl, as she gingerly circled Meg's leg with strips torn from a shirt. Will held the splint in place.

Meg, who had already felt a surge of adrenaline shoot out from her core to her extremities as if she had been given a powerful drug, responded truthfully that it was manageable. Her rational mind told her that this would be so until she moved. With all her heart she wished she could be anyplace right that moment but in a wet gully on a mountain with a broken leg.

Sam's raised voice made them all look up. "Sam," shouted Lenore, "leave Elsie be. Come on back and help us figure out how to get Meg out of here." Momentarily Sam reappeared.

"I've got that figured out," he said. "Remember the Forest Service ranger we saw this morning? With any luck he'll still be working at the cabin. He said he wanted to finish the job today. We'll have to get Meg back up on Lady Mischief, and Will and I will take turns leading her out. The cabin is halfway back, and once we alert McCray there'll be three of us to help get out to his truck on the Blue Ridge Parkway."

Meg chimed in with a weak attempt at humor, "I can tell you one thing, I may have led my horse down this trail, but I'm not leading him back up." Her teeth began to chatter involuntarily from the wet chill of the ground beneath her.

Watching this, Stanley leaned towards Sam and said, "You need to get underway; she could be going into shock."

Meg stiffened. "I may have a broken leg, but my hearing is fine. I am NOT going into shock, NOT now, and NOT while we're getting out of here. Let's get this show on the road. Where is Lady Mischief?"

"I'll get her," Stanley hastily volunteered.

He returned leading Meg's horse. Lady Mischief seemed to recognize that something was wrong, for with her rider prone on the ground in front of her, she didn't sidestep left or right but stood very still, as if aware of the gravity of the situation.

Contrary to the usual way of mounting, they positioned Lady Mischief to Meg's left. Sarah held the horse, while Lenore stood on her left side, prepared to position Meg's good leg in the stirrup when she reached the saddle.

Stanley, Sam, and Will, standing over Meg on Lady Mischief's other side, rehearsed how they would go about protecting Meg's bad leg. "I'll lift her bad leg," said Will, "if you two can get her torso in the saddle and her good leg over the pommel."

All this preparation was making Meg nervous. "Let's just get on with it. I can help a little, I think."

With that, they all moved together, rolling Meg onto her left hip before lifting her, leaning away from the pain, into the saddle. Her left foot quickly found the stirrup Lenore was holding for her—a natural movement most riders can do in their sleep—but as soon as she felt a shock of pain she looked down at her right leg and foot and blanched as she saw what was causing it. Her right foot had no connection to her leg except for the muscles, nerves and blood vessels running between the two. It flopped to the right, dangling sickeningly from the bottom of her leg.

"Oh God," exclaimed Will, "we're going to have to put that foot in the stirrup to keep it from fishtailing." As he gently lifted her toes toward the stirrup, Meg let out a scream of pain that stopped him. Still holding the front of the foot, he looked up at his wife questioningly. "Can you stand it if I try again? I can't think of anything else to protect it."

"NO," Meg replied, and he didn't argue with her. "Just let it hang," she ordered. "I can deal with that."

With extreme care Will lowered the foot until it hung unsupported. The men tried not to look at the unnatural angle it assumed. Sam took Lady Mischief's reins from Sarah as he said to Will, "I'll take the first shift leading if you get on Geronimo and come behind us lead-lining Rebel Yell."

"O.K." replied Will, as he went to get the horses.

"Lisl," ordered Sam, you're in charge." With a disgusted nod back at Elsie he continued, "She won't be any help; she's gone AWOL. But once you get there she should snap out of it and help with the routine. I'll get back as soon as I can. You know how to get to the church. Hobble the horses in the clearing so they can graze. You should be fine."

He gave her a last, fierce look and then turned and began leading Lady Mischief up the trail. Cries of "good luck" and "hang in there, Meg" followed them as Will, on horseback now, passed them, leading Rebel Yell as he caught up to Sam and Meg.

TEN

WILL AND SAM SAID LITTLE, INTENT on riding and walking out, and were attuned to Meg, who was hunched over in the saddle, using her arms propped against Lady Mischief's neck to take some of the weight off her leg. She tried not to look at her foot, dangling at a rakish angle that sometimes caught in bushes occasionally intruding on the trail.

The first time her foot brushed a branch, Meg said urgently, in a voice husky with pain, "My foot cannot touch ANYTHING. NOTHING. LESS THAN NOTHING." Will grimaced, and Sam took pains to stay as much as he could to the left of the narrow trail.

Meg talked to Lady Mischief as a way of making the time pass, telling her what was ahead in their path, patting her neck, urging her on. Meg's horse recognized the situation as unusual; she seemed to her rider to put her hooves down with extra care, trying to make the ride as smooth as possible.

"Sam," called Will after a half-hour or so, "why don't we switch places, and I'll lead and you ride for a while?"

"O.K." answered Sam, "we're about half-way to the cabin."

As they switched, Will put a hand on Meg's good leg and asked, "How are you doing?"

"I'm doing," said Meg, trying to smile as she looked down at him. "If you can just keep my foot from touching anything, I'll make it."

"I'll do my damndest," Will promised, taking Lady Mischief's reins.

The cabin was down a short path from the trail they were on, so Sam rode down to find McCray, Geronimo ambling along behind him, while Will and Meg waited at the junction. In no time they came back up the trail, with McCray loping ahead of them, throwing his empty backpack over his shoulders and securing the front waist clip.

Meg's face brightened as she saw him. "You are a sight for sore eyes," she exclaimed, "and when I see your truck that will be an even better sight!"

McCray came around to her right side and visibly reacted when he saw her foot paying no attention to her leg.

"Let's get you out of here," he responded calmly. "They'll know what to do with this at the Waynesboro Hospital."

"How far is that?" queried Meg.

"Oh, no distance—maybe five miles once we get to the truck, and we should reach that in a half-hour."

They decided that McCray could help most by walking on Lady Mischief's right side, helping to keep the brambles away from Meg's foot. For the first time that afternoon, Meg felt the tension lessening, even though the pain was a constant. Having someone else to help made a big difference.

Meg felt grateful that McCray didn't seem to need to hear a blow-by-blow. Each of them concentrated on his part of the job of getting her out to the parkway. She felt weirdly disconnected from the little world that was the four of them moving through the jungle-like growth on the mountain, as if she were looking down on it from an even higher mountain. This made it easier for her to concentrate not on the accident, but on the trail ahead.

Halfway to the intersection with the parkway, the trail emerged from the forest and entered an area where it went through a section of dense, waist-high bushes. The bushes crowded in closer to the riders, making the job of keeping Meg's foot untouched more difficult. As they negotiated their way through, Meg realized that she was hearing a new sound, a low persistent thrum.

Just as her mind began to register that it would take a lot of something to make such a sound, the first swarm of infuriated bees arose from the bushes and settled on the intruders. Within seconds horses and riders had been stung, and the horses' natural flight reaction had taken over. Lady Mischief, in the lead, took off, pulling Will along as he tried desperately to hang onto the reins. McCray, off-balance on her flank, was thrown into the bushes, and there was no protection for Meg's right foot.

"JESUS CHRIST," Meg yelled as her foot bounced uncontrollably, "HOLD ON, WILL." As they cleared the area of the bees, Lady Mischief finally tired of dragging Will along, and slowed to a stop. She stomped in place, impatient with the pain, and corkscrewed around to get at a bite on her flank. McCray and Sam, coming up behind them, hadn't fared any better. McCray had twice as many stings as anyone else, and Sam had a bad rope burn on his hand from trying to stop the riderless Geronimo from bolting past Rebel Yell.

Meg looked down at her right foot. It was still now, but her heart went icy when she saw blood on the cotton of Lisl's torn up tee shirt that they had used to splint her leg.

"Oh Meg," said Will, his eyes following hers, "the fracture has come through the skin." All of them knew that had this been a hundred years earlier, it would have been a death knell. As it was, it meant that they needed to get her to the hospital quickly so antibiotics could be started.

"Well, if Will hadn't hung on," said Meg, "I would have fallen off and been in an even worse pickle. Let's get the hell out of here before the seven-year locusts or the horsemen of the Apocalypse come out to get us."

Shaken and somber, they continued on the short distance

to the parkway, stepped out onto its grassy verge and, simultaneously, back into civilization. As McCray unlocked his truck and hastily threw the stuff on the front seat onto the floor in the rear of the cab, Sam told them the plan he had worked out in his mind.

"Will," he said, "after McCray has gotten Meg and you to the hospital, he'll call the farm and tell them what happened. You will need to tell my nephew, Tad, who is at the farm with Hans, what you would like him to bring you from the things you left behind at Whiskey Ridge. I'm going to wait here holding your two horses. Tad will hitch the trailer to our truck, come to the hospital in Waynesboro to deliver your things to you, and then come up here to pick up your two horses. After that I'll ride back and rejoin the group."

"That could be a long wait, Sam," said McCray, "especially if I can't reach them at the farm right away."

"I don't see any better plan, though," answered Sam, "do you?"

"Nope," came the reply.

"Are you ready, Meg, to transfer to this luxurious ambulance?" queried Will, full of relief that their journey out to the truck had ended, even as he worried about Meg's ashen face.

Now that they were at the truck, relief weakened Meg and she began to shake. She didn't answer, so Will and Sam lifted her out of the saddle while McCray made sure the right foot cleared the saddle without touching. They settled her in the backseat of the truck, with her foot resting on an old dog's bed that they had doubled over on itself.

Will climbed into the back of the truck from the driver's side as McCray wished Sam an easy trip getting back to the group. Then they pulled away, one man and three horses becoming smaller and smaller, receding into the background as McCray watched them in his rearview mirror.

Meanwhile, the diminished group of riders, led by Lisl on Stitch, had followed her orders and gotten on their horses instead of continuing to lead them. They made their way down the rest of the steep part of the trail without incident, preoccupied with their own thoughts. Once down, the way was straightforward: a mountain plateau widened out before them, and the valleys on either side receded.

There were more frequent small clearings, with gnarled apple trees and the occasional dry stonewall, put together without mortar, for penning a family milk cow or keeping a few goats. These were clues to the isolated homesteads that had been there a hundred years earlier. Less frequently a stone chimney still stood, testament to the log cabin it had once warmed.

In one such clearing Lisl spoke up, trying to override the grip that the accident had on the riders' minds. "Doesn't it fascinate you," she said, standing in her stirrups and twisting around to address the others, "to try to imagine who actually lived here a century ago? Was it a loner, making moonshine whiskey, a settler who was only here a few years before moving further west? Three generations of one family under one roof, scratching out a living up here? The possibilities are endless. I would give a lot to know."

To everyone's surprise, Elsie spoke up from the back of the line, and it was clear she hadn't been listening to Lisl. "If he hadn't bragged, it never would have happened. I shivered when he said we hadn't had an accident in ten years. The devil hears that kind of talk."

Stunned that she had spoken at all, much less three whole sentences, no one answered. Lenore considered, and then decided against, saying that she didn't believe in superstition. After Elsie had delivered this opinion, she seemed to retreat back into her own world.

Everyone was relieved when they arrived at the clearing that held the long-ago-de-sanctified Blue Ridge Chapel. It was hard enough for them to imagine the individuals who had lived where they were riding, but harder still to comprehend this evidence of their communal life together.

Sensing this, Lisl commented, "There was a real community up here, and churches didn't just serve as churches. They were community centers after the service on Sunday. If you came a long way to worship, then you stayed around to share a meal, have afternoon games for the children and socials for the adults, ending with a hymn sing before the trip home.

"Well, we're here," she continued, "and I think our timing is good, because it looks as if rain is coming. I don't expect Sam until much later, since he may have to wait awhile for Hans and Tad to come pick up the horses. If you all would take off the tack and help get our gear inside, I'll come around and hobble the horses, and Elsie and I will get started on supper." Everyone seemed relieved to return to the now-familiar routine.

The chapel was a welcome sight, even though only a few streaks of white were still visible on its weathered clapboard exterior. The bell tower atop it was slightly askew, and the bell long ago had lost its clapper. The site of the chapel was in the upper far corner of the clearing, opposite where they had ridden in.

A small stream they later learned was called Settlers' Creek ran from above the chapel down the hillside that formed the southern boundary of the clearing and on back into the woods at the bottom. On the bank below the chapel stood a tall lone Sycamore tree, its exposed root system cascading over the bank and into its water source, which explained its size and dominance.

Sometime after the chapel's life as a church, someone had added a roofed porch, an incongruous but comfortable addition. In no time their tack had been stacked on the porch, and they pushed open the simple door leading inside. At the far end, opposite the door, was a raised platform where the chancel had once been. Surprisingly, the chapel still had its windows, although a few panes were missing.

It had a painted pressed tin ceiling, which darkened the interior and lent it a feeling of heaviness, as if the ceiling would at any moment come down to meet the old heart pine floor. The one large room was stripped of furniture, with the exception of a warped table with a few ladder-back wooden chairs around it and a useable potbellied stove.

Lenore and Stanley went out to gather firewood in the forest just behind the chapel. Old growth maples and oaks on the upper verge of the clearing were magnificent trees that had benefitted from a logger's unwillingness to log an area so near Holy Hollow, as the spot was called.

Away from the others, they were eager for a chance to talk, so they sat on a downed log in the forest, out of the hearing of those on the porch or in the chapel. Lenore began, "Is this a strange group on a strange trip, or is it just the effect of Meg's accident on me?"

"No," Stanley answered, "your instincts are right. It's an age-old story—Sam is just trying to do too much with too little. His operation runs on a shoestring, for God knows what reason his wife is a basket case, without Lisl he'd be up a creek, and preparation for emergencies is non-existent. Only the horses are top notch, which is lucky."

"Do you think Meg will be able to make it on the way out?" Lenore mused, arching her back with her hands on her waist to get the kinks out.

"I think so," Stanley said. "She looked pretty determined to get out of these mountains, and when they pick up McCray and head for his truck, she'll take heart, I'll bet."

"Yeah," agreed Lenore, "he looked like a pretty dependable guy.

"I don't know, though," she went on. "I'd figured this would be an easy article to write, plus the trip being a vacation for the two of us. But the article is getting complicated because I'm not sure I'd want to recommend this trip to anyone. Plus, this is seeming more like work than a vacation."

Stanley lifted his upper torso with his arms and slid down closer to her on the log. Putting one arm around her, he hugged her. "Well," he countered, recognizing the worry in his wife's voice, "the article won't lack for drama, anyway."

She turned to look at him and saw that he was smiling at her. She felt herself relax as she put both arms around his chest and returned his hug.

Count on Stanley to look at the bright side, she thought to herself. He was like the little boy who, looking in his stocking one Christmas and finding it full of manure, immediately beams and says, "I got a pony!" As it had so many times before, his positive attitude made her fears seem silly.

They got up, grabbed the pieces of wood they had collected, and headed back to the chapel. As they emerged from the woods into the clearing, a few drops of rain began to fall.

ELEVEN

Sam woke with a start, stumbling forward a step on a foot that had no feeling in it. He had been leaning against Geronimo when fatigue caught him. His foot had gone to sleep so thoroughly while he dozed that it wouldn't hold him upright, and he fell over, cursing. The three horses, startled, raised their heads, snorted and moved back from him, but their reins were still in his hands and Sam held on to them.

For a moment he wondered what he was doing here as the shadows lengthened, holding three horses, but then it all came flooding back to him—the afternoon, the accident, what he was waiting for.

"I don't blame you for wondering what we're doing here," he said, addressing the startled horses in a soothing tone. "For all I know we may be here for the night, if for some reason McCray didn't get hold of Tad. I wish he'd show up so you and I, Rebel, can make our way to Holy Hollow while there's still some light in the sky."

Reassured by his tone, the horses went back to the position they'd been in all afternoon, heads drooping, weight on three legs, one rear hoof turned up, resting. Wide-awake now, Sam heard his stomach make a serious rumble. I was stupid not to put some food in my knapsack, he thought to himself. I would give a lot for even a dry piece of bread about now.

He was trying to get the thought of food out of his head when he heard the familiar motor of his own pickup truck. Looking up, he saw it come around the bend toward him with two figures in the front seat, the stock trailer rattling along behind.

Tad made a wide turn across the parkway and drew up behind Sam and the horses. Both Tad and Hans jumped out as soon as the truck stopped.

"Sorry, Sam," said Tad, "we came as soon as we could, but Hans was using the truck to pull the manure spreader, and it took us a while to switch the spreader for the trailer."

"That's O.K.," Sam said. "We figured it would take a while. But now I'm really in a hurry to hand Lady Mischief and Geronimo over to you two. I've got to use what daylight there is left to try to get back to the others at Holy Hollow tonight."

With that he handed their reins over to Tad, put his own reins over Rebel Yell's head and his foot in the stirrup, and settled himself in his saddle. For an instant, his stiff body yearned to trade his horse for the truck and the certainty of a scalding shower and his own bed, but he banished the thought before it could blossom.

Concern in his face, Hans moved to the side of Rebel Yell. Putting his hand on the reins to restrain horse and rider for one instant, he spoke hesitantly, looking up at Sam.

"Lisl is how?" he began.

Sam responded impatiently, "Lisl? She's not the problem. Meg is the problem. She broke her leg badly. I've got to go—stop slowing me down." With that he kicked Rebel Yell, reluctant to leave his stable-mates, into a fast trot, and they disappeared off the verge of the parkway and into the woods.

"Rats," exclaimed Tad, "I forgot to give him the ham sandwich we brought along. He was in such a hurry it wiped it out of my mind. Oh well, let's load up these two and get on back for our own supper." He reached into the front seat of the truck to get the sandwich and gave half of it to Hans.

Eating with one hand and leading the horses with the other, they loaded Lady Mischief and Geronimo and took off for Whiskey Ridge.

As Sam urged Rebel Yell back down the trail dusk was thickening around him, and at the same time threatening clouds seemed to be rolling up into the sky, a roiling mass not moving west to east, as usually happened. As daylight waned he let Rebel Yell walk; the horse's head hung slightly as he picked his way around the rocks and stones.

As he passed the turnoff for the rangers' cabin, he wondered fleetingly if he shouldn't stop there for the night, but it wasn't yet raining and he felt it would be possible to make it to the church safely if he didn't push Rebel Yell.

Now that Meg was in the hands of the doctors, Sam began to worry about the group ahead of him. Lisl would of course have taken charge. Had Elsie snapped out of her private world? Would Sarah, Lenore and Stanley be comfortable enough with the routine to help out? The church wasn't the most glamorous lodging in the world, but at least they had a roof over their heads.

Just then it began to rain gently. Darkness approached, and Sam cursed his decision a half-hour before not to spend the night in the cabin. It wasn't long before the rain picked up in intensity and, more worryingly, lightning struck to the south, followed by the growl of thunder.

As he moved along through the dripping darkness, dependent on a four-legged animal whose sight and sense of smell were so much better than his own, he had the sensation of being a pawn in a chess game. It was as if, at any moment, a cosmic hand might reach down from the sky, pick up Rebel Yell and himself, and put them in a different place on the playing board that was this mountain landscape.

With a chill he felt that this would not be a benevolent move, it would have no rationale, it would just be the mindless whim of a malevolent force. Sam felt that force, looking down from a great height, eyeing him with the same stealth and playful disregard as a cat determining when to pounce on a mouse. He became aware that he was doubled over in the saddle, hunched against Rebel Yell's neck, as if to avoid that invisible hand.

While he was straightening up in the saddle to ward off this thought, the arc of a bolt of lightning revealed a trail leading down to his left. He knew where it led—it was a path down to a rock outcropping that lent a breathtaking view in the daylight out over the Rockfish Valley. At its top, a large rock jutted out of the side of the mountain at an angle that made it a natural roof for someone standing under it. The rocks were surrounded by bushes and trees taller and more robust than those on the crest of the mountain. They would provide some protection against the wind and the rain.

This shelter would have to do for tonight, he decided, thankful that the lightning had come at such an opportune moment. Rebel Yell was beyond objecting when Sam neck-reined him onto the descending trail. They picked their way down carefully, and Sam realized the distance was farther than he thought. Eventually the dark mass of the overhang appeared on their right, and Sam brought Rebel Yell to a halt. As fast as he could, he pulled off his saddle and pack and put them under the shelter of the overhang, flinging his bridle on top as soon as he could exchange it for the halter.

"Sorry, my boy," Sam said to Rebel Yell as he led him away from the rocks, "there's not room enough for two of us under there, and I don't have any feed for you either. 'Fraid we're both in for a long night."

After stumbling around in a patch of huckleberry bushes, he located a tree with a low branch, and tied the lead line to it. There was no point in hobbling Rebel Yell as there was no grass for the horse to graze on anywhere nearby.

Rebel Yell moved his rear end around so that it took the brunt of the rain, plastered his ears to his head and looked the picture of dejection. As soon as Sam took a few steps away toward the overhang, he could no longer see the horse, so complete was the darkness.

Sam moved his saddle and pack behind him and leaned back against them. The dampness brought out the smell of his horse, a scent he had always liked. His torso was elevated enough to look out at the tracery of rain water just beginning to come over the lip of the ledge projecting out above his head.

He was trying not to think about how hungry he was, and realized if he hadn't been in such a hurry, Tad and Hans probably would have given him some food from the truck. Missing one meal was one thing, but missing two in a row catapulted hunger into a new category.

He thumped the pockets of his oilskin raincoat, feeling for any little bump that might mean food.

"Aha!" he said to himself as he fingered a square of plastic in an inside pocket. Carefully he pulled it out, as if he were removing a gold coin from buried sea treasure. It turned out to be a little package of saltine crackers, broken into pieces, but still food. Triumphantly he held it up, puzzling over how to eat its contents without spilling the crumbs. Slowly he tore the plastic opening, held his head back, and dumped the contents into his mouth.

The saltiness of the crackers made him thirsty, so he untied his canteen from the saddle and drank some water. As he sat there in the steady sound of the rain, exhaustion took over and his body gradually relaxed into the side of the saddle and the hard rock beneath him. He closed his eyes and gave in to sleep.

Discomfort and unease combined to wake Sam sometime after midnight. What first caught his attention was the roar caused by the volume of water coming over the rock in front of him. When he had gone to sleep, it had been a bridal veil waterfall, a series of small streams of water making their way over the ledge, along the dozen or so feet of overhang above his head.

Now it was a solid sheet of water, like a gigantic tub turned on its side, ceaselessly overflowing. It made Sam's few square feet of flat rock into a deafening cell, imprisoning him in his own distorted world.

The only sound that penetrated the roar of the waterfall was thunder, following hard on the heels of lightning strike after lightning strike. Sam got on his feet and went to the edge of the curtain of water in front of him. From there, when lightning exposed his confined world for a few seconds, Rebel Yell's image seared itself into his mind. The young horse was still tied, but was frantically moving his hind end from side to side, rotating around his almost immobile head.

In normal circumstances Sam would have gone down to his horse to calm him, but not in this maelstrom. Being a farmer, Sam was used to gauging the strength of rain, and he knew instinctively that he could not stand up to it.

Besides, he thought to himself, what would you do when you got to him? No stall to put him into, no field to turn him out in—both of us will just have to make do. The worst that could happen, he thought, was that Rebel Yell would break his halter, run away, and be the devil to catch after the storm.

So Sam moved to the middle of his rocks, squarely under the protection of the overhang, and prepared to wait the storm out. Even though it wasn't raining on him directly, it seemed to him that the world had turned to water. Gusts blew it horizontally across in front of him, and the very air he breathed seemed heavy with moisture. At the same time that he knew himself to be lucky to be under the overhang, he felt trapped on his ledge, a prisoner of the natural world.

He didn't go back to sleep, but into a kind of trance, where he felt apart from the wet chill and the roar of the rain. In the search of his pockets he'd also come up with wool gloves and a neck gaiter, which he put on, grateful for their warmth. He considered praying, and decided against it. Why should he pray to God, who was presumably the one to have gotten him into this predicament?

He had no sense of the passage of time. Gradually, however, it dawned on him that although the rain was as intense as ever, the lightning strikes had abated. If the thunderstorm has moved on, he thought to himself, why is it still raining so hard?

He realized he had never seen rain come down like this. Was this what it had been like for Noah? He must also have felt like the last surviving human on the earth. At least, Sam reflected, Noah had God telling him what to do.

From the left side of the outcropping came the familiar sound of thunder, low at first and from up above him, but then deepening and advancing nearer. Sam stood, alert and listening, for he was sure he had not seen lightning.

Suddenly a rotten smell clogged his head, a smell he did not recognize. It was penetrating, earthy, musty in a way that stirred the stomach in rebellion. It was coming from humus, soil that had not seen the light of day for centuries, rich from the work of worms and the biological processes of decay over the ages.

As he moved to the edge to look out, the rumbling was now deafening, like the sound the motors of transcontinental jets make revving their engines before take off. As he looked up the slope he could just make out the shapes of trees moving downward.

In the absurd shifts that the mind makes when faced with things it can't explain, Sam's memory reverted to his Shakespeare course at Virginia Tech. Has Burnam Wood come to Dunsinane? His befuddled brain asked itself. Then, just as absurdly, if the noise were from one big tree falling over, I wouldn't still be hearing it.

Seconds later, his mind went blank as the rocks under him shook. Upright trees, boulders, and bushes slid by him on a mass of liquefied sub-soil that had given up its tenuous hold on the ancient bedrock of the Blue Ridge Mountains.

"Oh Jesus, Rebel Yell!" he screamed into the teeth of the wholesale destruction of the world around him. As the scream left his mouth, the words seemed to double back into him. He was too late. If he had left his perch, he would be dead too.

But his powerlessness galled him. Tears streamed down his face at the thought of Rebel Yell, helpless and terrified, being swept up in that lethal cauldron of mud and the instruments of destruction within it. He would be crushed to death as if he were a toy horse that a perverse child threw into a disposal, instead of the terrorized, thousand-pound animate creature being drawn into that moving mass of mountainside that had given way.

Sam stood still, transfixed, not at all sure what he had witnessed. First, it was still dark, so the possibility was there that this was the end of the world. Trying to grope backwards from catastrophe into rational thought, he reminded himself that the disaster had been confined to his left flank; nothing seemed to have taken place in the dark to his right. Following this line of thinking, he figured so much rain had fallen onto already saturated soil that earth above him had given way and was taking anything in its path with it.

The continuous thunder it generated was still audible, but well below him now. Sam was gripped by the need to see—what was gone, what was left—and wished he could arbitrarily declare that the new day come immediately. In it lay his only hope of getting back to any semblance of the existence he remembered as short a time ago as yesterday.

But tomorrow was taking its own good time, and before long, Sam for the third time gave in to exhaustion. Hungry, tired, wet, cold, and with his mind in tumult, he collapsed against his saddle and tried not to think of Rebel Yell.

TWELVE

As Lenore and Stanley walked downhill, carrying the firewood they had collected from the forest above, they both gasped when they reached the clearing and saw the movement in the sky above them. Full daylight had waned to dusk and bad weather was clearly on the way, but something else, something they had never seen before, was happening to the clouds.

Dark gray masses were bubbling upwards and fulminating at the top of the heavens. It looked for all the world like a devil's brew, working itself up from bottom to top to put a spell on the land underneath it. Lenore shuddered involuntarily. Most thunderstorms, she thought, hunkered down as they blossomed, moving in a horizontal sweep across the landscape.

"Maybe," she said to Stanley, "this is a mountain phenomenon. Let's see what Lisl and Elsie think." Stanley said nothing, which was unlike him, but his eyes were riveted skyward. They stepped onto the porch, put some of the firewood down and took the rest inside.

"Elsie, Lisl, Sarah: come quickly and look at the sky."

All five piled out the door, down the porch steps and out into the clearing. The three who had been in the chapel were silenced by what they saw.

"Is this normal for this part of the world?" Lenore asked. Elsie remained silent, her thoughts so deep within her there was no way of even guessing what she might be thinking. Lisl looked for some time before she spoke, carefully.

"No, I've never seen cloud formations like that, here or at home in Switzerland." Then her cautious tone changed. In a brighter voice she said, "Let's go in and make a good fire with the wood Stanley and Lenore collected. Elsie and I will make supper. Aren't we glad not to be camping out tonight?"

Lenore bit her tongue not to say she'd rather be back home in her own house. Stanley looked at her sideways, guessing exactly what she was thinking.

As they started back toward the chapel, the few drops of rain had turned into a light drizzle. The inside of the chapel, which had seemed so plain and unkempt before, was such a welcome haven when they went back in. Elsie lit the kerosene lanterns, setting one on the step up to what used to be the chancel of the church, and the other in the middle of the rickety table.

Lisl brought in kindling wood and laid the fire, putting leftover paper from food wrappings between the kindling and the logs. Everyone was cheered when the match caught immediately. Elsie put the pasta water on to boil and set about opening the jars of marinara sauce that were to go with it.

Lenore chopped celery and carrots for the salad, and Sarah was slathering butter on the loaf of Italian bread. Stanley busied himself setting the wobbly table, folding squares of paper towels over to make them look like napkins. Everyone took comfort in these routine domestic duties, as it took their minds off the storm.

Lisl, working alongside Elsie, blushed as she thought of Sam. Where was he now? Was he as obsessed with her as she was with him? Would he make it back to them tonight? Did he have any food? She must save a portion of tonight's meal for him, if Elsie didn't.

How was he managing in the dark and the rain, and why hadn't he arrived yet? She yearned with her whole being for him to come striding through that door, and she blushed again as her body remembered the previous night, which now seemed eons ago.

The conversation around the table in the low light of the lamps was desultory, at least until Lenore threw out, "Let's go round the table and each describe a typical day in our normal, at-home lives. It will help us know each other much better than we do now."

No one objected, so Lisl said, "Why don't you start, Lenore."

Lenore thought a minute and then said, "Well, early morning is a deliberate routine in our household. Our son has Down syndrome, so Stanley and I work hard to keep things on an even keel before we all leave the house. Roddy likes to know in advance exactly what he is going to be doing, so we describe the day ahead and try not to be rushed about it. Claire, our daughter, is good about collecting the things she needs for the day—her ballet slippers, her schoolbooks—and she makes lunch for herself and her brother.

"We live in the country but near my office at *The Chronicle of the Horse*. Stanley has a long commute, all the way into Arlington, but he doesn't have to be at work until 10 a.m. He drops the children off at school, and I pick them up in the afternoon.

"I love my work, but it's lucky I'm not the only breadwinner. I've been at the *Chronicle* long enough now so that, even though I'm an editor, I can suggest subjects for articles and write them myself. I spend most of the day, though, editing the work of others, including free-lancers, who often send in articles."

"What kinds of articles?" Sarah asked. "Does the *Chronicle* specialize in one particular equine discipline?"

"No," answered Lenore, "but the emphasis is definitely on fox-hunting and racing on the East Coast.

"We also occasionally do travel articles. Once we had a free-lancer who sent in an article about riding up-country in the Ivory Coast in West Africa. She sent pictures, too, and they were mounted on the scrawniest gray nags you've ever seen, not much bigger than ponies, with all their ribs showing, but, apparently, they were very hardy. The women riding them said they felt sorry for the horses the whole time!

"I'm going on too long. At the end of a typical day, I'm the taskmaster at home, overseeing homework, making dinner, etc. I feed the children early, and then when Stanley gets home we have a late dinner, pour ourselves some wine and unwind for the day. That's about it."

Stanley jumped in after his wife. "We have a wonderful life, living in the country, but the commute is our payment for it. I'm an architect, specializing in adaptive reuse for old buildings, so I'm in close touch with historical societies and realtors who specialize in old houses, warehouses and old factories. Business is fine at the moment, but it can get lean and mean according to how the economy is doing and depending on whether federal and state governments are offering tax credits for these rehab jobs."

"What would you consider your favorite rehab, Stanley?" asked Sarah.

He didn't hesitate in answering, "Our house, which spent its first one hundred years as a barn. We're lucky, in that the pasture it is in is on a slope. The front of the structure that you drive up to now looks like the front of a house, except that the old attached silo gives it away.

"We live on that entrance floor, with the two children's bedrooms in what used to be the old hayloft. The level below the main floor you can get to only from outside. The entrance is on the other side from the house entrance. It is still a barn that opens out into the slope of the pasture going down to a pond we can swim in during the summer and ice skate on at least once or twice during the winter.

"We keep two horses, chickens, and a Vietnamese potbel-lied pig named Rufus. The children take care of the chickens and gather the eggs. They have a good little business selling them."

"Oh," exclaimed Sarah, "that is so different from the big city life I lead. I'm jealous!"

"Well then, come visit us on your next vacation, why don't you," volunteered Lenore. "And tell us about London and the Foreign Service. That must be fascinating work."

"Well," said Sarah, "it can be, but it can also be a terrible bore. The big embassies are so much about entertaining; so many artists, businessmen, performers, scientists, you name it, come to town, and someone my age, with as little seniority as I have, often has to go to these parties, and I don't mean during work hours. That's how they get sixty work hours out of us in a forty-hour work week.

"When my two years are up, I'm going to try for a post-ing to a small, less-important country with a smaller embassy. That way, hopefully, I'll be in a job with more responsibility. This is the stage in my life when I can go anywhere, so I'm gunning for Thailand, or Morocco. Later on I'd love to be posted to India."

"Do you think you'll stay in the Foreign Service for your whole career?" queried Lisl.

"That depends - - - on who I meet, and whether or not I think I'm getting a fair shake at postings and job assignments. I don't have a boyfriend at the moment, but I'm always on the lookout," she said, smiling. "My mother would love it if I left the service immediately, but that isn't gonna happen."

"What kinds of things do you do during the day?" asked Lenore.

"I'm a third secretary," said Sarah, "which is pretty low on the totem pole. At the moment I'm sort of a jack-of-all-trades. Some days I might be working on a visa problem, or following up on a call for help from a visitor who has had her pocketbook stolen with all her travelers' checks and passport in it. Or I might be delegated to go to Heathrow to meet, say, the Smith College Glee Club or the Alvin Ailey Dance Group coming to England on a tour.

"My job is to welcome them, escort them to their hotel, see that there are no problems with their check-in, and give my name and number to the leaders so they can reach me if they hit a snag during their visit. I guess you would call me a facilitator. What I like about my job is that no two days are the same, and almost every day I trade my office for the streets, so boredom is not a problem."

As Sarah finished, the little group around the table became aware of the noise from the rain, which was steady and hard, its stiletto effect on the tin roof picking up in tempo.

Sarah turned to Elsie, who was sitting beside her. "Elsie, tell us what your day is like if you're not taking us riders out."

Immediately Elsie pushed back her chair. "I'm going to get us some dessert," was all she said, heading back to the stove to retrieve the warming bread pudding she'd made at home.

Lenore chimed in, "We know what Elsie does most every day: she works!" The others laughed and agreed, and greeted the arrival of the bread pudding with enthusiasm.

"How about you, Lisl?" prompted Sarah.

"Oh, compared to Sarah's, my job in Switzerland is very boring," responded Lisl. "I didn't go to university, but I do have an International Baccalaureate degree, and that qualified me to work for a group of local lawyers. I manage their office, file papers for them, act as a secretary, do some basic research for them, remind them of vital things like their wives' birthdays...It's not a job that I'd want to do for long, but it suits at this stage of my life."

Lisl was just wrestling with whether or not to delve into the subject of her love for horses and how satisfying she found working with them to be, when she realized she could hardly talk over what was now a roar coming from outside.

The sound of rain coming down, no matter how hard, could not be solely responsible for the din. Just at that moment Stanley, who had gotten up to scrape his plate into the plastic bag of garbage, reported, "We're beginning to get leaks; it's coming down in several places."

Lisl stood abruptly and with a new urgency in her voice said, "Elsie, let's you and me go out and check on the horses." Elsie signaled her willingness by leaving the dishes and pulling on her oilskin and hat. Lisl did the same, and reaching the door first, opened it.

Even though she had been in a hurry to get outside, what she saw when she opened the door caused her to stop dead in her tracks. Elsie, whose head was down, plowed into her, sending them both stumbling onto the porch.

"Dear God in heaven, look at that!" exclaimed Lisl. Elsie sucked in her breath and put a hand over her mouth. Lightning strikes had become almost constant, and the thunder that followed them sounded like rifle shots. By that cold, blue-white morticians' light they got glimpses of the whole clearing, like a theater's curtain that went up and then suddenly fell down. Before their eyes could adjust to the darkness, lightning would strike again.

Settlers' Creek, which two hours before had been a small stream perhaps three feet wide and six inches deep, had metastasized into a raging river, leaving its banks and hurtling down the slope, and then spreading itself across the relatively flat ground below the chapel in the clearing.

Lisl was mesmerized, looking at the hurtling tree branches, stones, and bushes that were churning along, propelled by the ever-increasing volume of water. Suddenly she realized that the care of these people and the horses was now her responsibility, and it seemed a crushing burden in the present circumstances. "Jesus Christ, Sam, where are you?" she muttered to herself.

In the next lightening flash Lisl managed to locate all the animals except the mules. Denise and DeNephew had two-legged hobbles tied on and could move about in them much better than the horses, who were tied up. The two mules had already hobbled their way up the hill into the forest and to higher ground.

Earlier, when she had tied on the hobbles, Lisl made Stitch the picket horse, the one whose movement was limited by the length of the line tied to a stake hammered into the ground. If one horse is picketed, it's more likely that the others will stay close by; horses are herd animals, ill at ease by themselves.

Because Stitch needed to get to water, Lisl had staked the picket close enough to the creek for the horse to drink. This made sense when she did it, but now Stitch was frantic, straining against the rope as far away from the creek as he could get, water already at his knees and rising more quickly than seemed possible.

Sassafras, Donegal and Packer had abandoned their friend and had managed to get most of the way across the clearing despite their hobbles. However, she had put Challenger in a three-legged hobble, as he was deviously clever at making tracks in the two-legged one, and, being an alpha horse, would lead them all astray.

"Elsie," Lisl cried out, "you go for Challenger and get his hobble off, and I'll get Stitch off the picket."

"O.K.," responded Elsie to Lisl's already retreating back.

Sarah, Stanley and Lenore had followed them to the porch and watched as the two women went toward the horses, bent double as they encountered what was no longer rainfall, but sheets of water that seemed determined to flatten them to the ground.

THIRTEEN

Lɪsʟ ᴛᴏᴏᴋ ᴏɴᴇ ʟᴀsᴛ ʟᴏᴏᴋ ɪɴ the flash of a lightning strike and made a beeline for the terrified Stitch. The frantic pony was thrusting his head from side to side in a vain attempt to loosen the picket.

Within seconds of leaving the protection of the porch, Lisl felt she couldn't breathe, such was the force of the wall of water coming down on her. Instinctively, she cupped her hand over her nose, and was able to gulp a few breaths. After half a minute of propelling herself down the hill and into the water on the flatter ground where the horses were, she looked up to locate Stitch. Maybe, she thought to herself, I've overrun her, so she stopped and waited for the next lightning strike.

When it came, she looked left, but could take in only Elsie, who had reached Challenger and was bending over his front legs. Lisl forced herself to wait again, this time for slightly longer.

"Come lightning, come NOW," she intoned, her free fist balled in frustration.

As if in response to her incantation, a particularly severe, close flash, with an almost instantaneous answering explosion of thunder, revealed Stitch to her right. The muddy swirling waters were up to the pony's belly, and she was thrashing wildly, trying to stay on her feet.

Try as she might, Lisl felt as if strong men were holding her back as she moved in agonizingly slow motion through the water towards Stitch. When she neared the pony she realized she would not be able to undo the lead line by which the pony was tied. Her only chance of freeing Stitch, Lisl realized, would be to pull out the picket.

For a moment she forgot about breathing, and putting both her arms around Stitch's neck to balance herself, she tried to reassure the pony that she was doing her best to release her. With her hands no longer free, she had to tuck her nose into the collar of her oilskin to be able to breathe.

For a brief few seconds, Stitch stopped struggling. Lisl used that time to move up to the pony's head and grab hold of the picket line. A moment before, she had had to fight down panic at how weak she had felt, fighting the force of the water to get to Stitch. Something in that panic must have set loose the adrenaline that hit her as if she had been given an injection. She could feel it coursing through her core, and out her arms and legs to her extremities.

Using the strength that came with it, Lisl pulled herself hand over hand up the line. After a few steps, she gave up trying to keep her feet on the ground, as it was easier to let the water take her body while she made slow headway up the rope.

Five minutes ago there had been brownish pools of water swirling out onto the meadow the horses had been grazing in, rising higher and higher but essentially moving horizontally, not vertically. Now, these pools were being incorporated into the current of an unrecognizable torrent in full flood stage, bent on reaching the valley, claiming everything in its path, and also much that no rational person would have ever considered to be in its path.

Had Lisl not had every nerve in her body focused on getting to that picket, she might have heard Elsie screaming at her to give it up and try to save herself. Had she looked up, she would have seen twenty-foot waves, with branches and rocks tumbling within the maelstrom only a few yards away. But she struggled on, managing most of the time to keep her head above water, her body strung out behind her like a mermaid's.

She had to stop, almost there. Her heart beat in her throat and head so fast and loud she felt as if her head would explode. Her lungs, starved for air, made her feel as she had once before when thrown from a horse onto her back on hard earth. Instead of being able to take in air, she could barely hold on for the spasmodic heaving that took its place.

Only the rising water got her going again. With one last lunge she reached the end of the line. Lisl knew that she had put the stake in on the straight vertical, since any picket driven into the earth on an angle will give way. She also knew that the best way to get it out was to position herself right over it.

As far as she could determine, she was now over it. So, with her last remnant of strength, she took the biggest breath she could manage and went underwater. To her surprise and great relief, one yank was all it took. Water had loosened the soil, and seconds later she bobbed to the surface, still clutching the stake.

Simultaneously she extended her legs, expecting to feel the ground beneath her. But there was no ground there, and terror gripped her as she realized that in setting Stitch free, she had catapulted both of them perilously close to the ever-widening vortex of cascading water to their right.

Stitch, the instant he felt his release, began swimming to the left, toward the uncertain safety of the meadow. Lisl felt that her only chance of reaching it as well was to get closer to the pony. Again she used the rope to pull herself up to Stitch, so worried about drowning that she was unaware that this extra drag on the struggling pony made it even more difficult for Stitch to get to standing ground.

By now Lisl had a hold on both the rope and the pony's tail, and it was evident that Stitch was tiring. A hoarse cry of

"Come on girl, you can make it," burst through Lisl's gritted teeth.

And the valiant pony might well have made it if fate hadn't intervened. A huge log, expelled from the main current, drifted in the swirling outer-waters; a scary and unidentifiable hulk between Stitch and Lisl and the meadow. It was a nursery log, so called because it had been dead for some time. New life, in the form of mosses, toadstools, and seedlings, had grown from it, giving it more mass—and a strange shape in the dark.

Stitch, out of her mind with fright, instinctively veered away from it, turning into the flow of the monstrous current. That was all it took to give the wall of water the upper hand, as the vortex sucked them in.

"NO, Stitch, NO!" screamed Lisl, but she was powerless to turn the pony, and her words were lost in the tumult.

🐎 🐎 🐎

The calm light of morning gradually penetrated under the overhang, the sun filtering in from the east, tentacles of light finally reaching Sam's inert body. During the night he had gone somewhere beyond mere sleep and into a semi-consciousness beyond dreams. Perhaps it is the body's way of shutting down the mind when it has been burdened with more than it can bear.

Hours after his day would have normally started, he became aware of light, but for long periods of time he didn't have the strength to push up into full consciousness. He was aware that he had reason not to want to wake up, but he couldn't remember what that was, so he would sink back down below the threshold of being awake, and more time would go by.

An indeterminate amount of time later, he stirred; as soon as he did, stiffness and pain accosted his body and spurred him into wakefulness. He waited a minute before making the effort to sit up. His neck ached from the odd angle of his head while he was sleeping, his old collarbone break was talking to him, and his back felt like a rusty coil from an old box spring.

He used both hands to slowly raise his upper body. What he saw when he reached a sitting position brought the horror of the night flooding back. In front of him yawned a lunar landscape that followed the V shape of the small hollow above and below the rock outcropping that had preserved his life. The sun was too bright. There were no oaks, beech or poplar trees to give shade, no more deadwood leftover from the old growth chestnut trees, no bushes to give huckleberries, no mountain laurel to bloom in the spring, no mosses, no fungi, no loose rocks or boulders, nothing; just light glinting off the ghostly bedrock, unseemly in its nakedness.

Sam felt as empty as the landscape in front of him. He turned his head to look to the right, where trees crouched, bent over from the storm, and dead branches littered the ground. This, he knew, was nature's severe pruning. The scene to his left bore no relationship to anything he had seen before in the natural world. It was as if the forces of good and evil fought a cosmic battle the night before, and evil had triumphed and then gone on a senseless rampage.

Sam was struck by his own insignificance. That he had lived to see it he knew, rationally, was remarkable, but something in him didn't want to acknowledge such an exhibit of raw power.

He had a premonition of what life would be like after being a witness to this random destruction. He felt tainted by an unwelcome understanding of what could happen, what he now knew was within the realm of possibility. He felt he was seeing with new eyes, and he didn't like it.

He got to his feet, took off his oilskin, and for the first time in twelve hours, left his perch on the ledge below the overhang. Moving slowly and cautiously, grabbing hold of branches to break his speed while sidestepping down the grade parallel to the denuded slope, he could think only of Rebel Yell, hoping that he died of a massive traumatic injury—from a boulder, maybe—early in the slide; that he didn't survive long in that jumbled mass avalanching off the mountainside.

Suddenly he arrested himself. He knew that subconsciously he was looking for Rebel—as if the handsome bay might just appear out of the woods, miraculously unscathed, nickering for a carrot, nuzzling Sam's pocket where he knew it was hidden.

The image was so strong that, for the first time, he broke down and sobbed, standing there looking at the bleak landscape, knowing that nothing living survived that slide. There was no point in continuing downhill. The severe grade of the slope meant that the momentum of the slide would have pushed anything before it down to the valley. Rebel was not going to appear out of the woods.

As he walked back up the slope, worry about the rest of the group muscled its way into his mind and replaced grief for his horse. Sam's pace picked up as his thoughts turned to wondering how the five of them had fared. They must have made the safety of the old chapel, he thought, since they had a big head start on him.

In his mind he recreated the topography of Holy Hollow, and was glad when he remembered that the slope in the woods above it was not as steep as where he had ended up for the night.

How had the chapel held up, he wondered? Lisl, he felt sure, would have taken charge. The horses would certainly have had a miserable night. The creek! Oh God, the creek! A sense of doom came over him as he remembered the intensity and the duration of the rain the night before. And the hobbled horses! He began to scramble faster up the mountain. His mind raced. Lisl will have endangered herself to save those horses, he thought to himself.

No sooner had this thought struck than he felt a stab of guilt that Lisl's safety meant so much more to him than Elsie's. "I've got to get there," he said aloud, as he stepped back onto his ledge. He looked at his watch. It was 10 a.m.; he had no horse, and would need to walk at a fast pace to get there by mid-afternoon.

His mind moved ahead to the rest of the trip, and then it occurred to him that he couldn't lead the trip without a horse. Worse, a creeping consciousness settled over him that what he found at the chapel might be worse than what he had witnessed here. If he took his tack with him it would slow him considerably, and the important thing now was to show up.

Leaving his saddle and bridle right where they were under the protection of the overhang, he climbed back up to the ridge of the mountain and set off toward the southwest on the trail, headed for Holy Hollow.

FOURTEEN

As Lisl and Stitch disappeared from the landscape into the muddy, roiling waves, she thought to herself, "If I am going to die, let it happen quickly." But it didn't happen quickly; after a minute of being pushed under the surface, thrust upwards again and muscled sideways by debris, a violent will to live took hold of her.

She still had a tight grip on Stitch's tail; wherever the heavier pony went, she followed. Lisl tried to make her body limp, even as her arms were taut with the effort of gripping the tail. Stitch's tail was long, which kept her from running into his churning back legs.

A small log shot into the air from the turmoil behind her and came down on the back of her left leg, above the back of the knee, at a moment when she was on the surface of the water. The pain was sharp, but she hardly registered it; she was so intent on surviving. The pony was her lifeline.

She was dimly aware that the greatest danger came from huge trees pulled up by their roots in the force of the current and toppled over nearly intact into the maelstrom. One had fallen over from the left side several yards in front of Stitch and so far was moving perpendicular to the current, with half its branches riding above water.

Just as the goal of grabbing a limb formed in her mind, she was able to make out that the base of the tree ahead had snagged on a massive boulder at the start of a curve to the left. The boulder domed perhaps a foot above the water, but the larger waves washed over its top. Its flat side faced upstream. It was so big that it had withstood the current, and everything that came from upstream had to contend with it.

This flood was creating one thousand years' worth of topographical change in one night. But as rampaging Settlers' Creek continued to seek the fastest, straightest route downwards, the curve that had existed until that night still dictated that debris coming from upstream was pulled down onto the boulder.

The root base of the tree was hung up on the boulder, but the influence of the current had swung the big sycamore around so that its trunk and branches were closer to parallel with the current. Their leafy mass choked the main channel to the right of the rock.

Lisl saw what the boulder had done to reroute the tree and thought to herself, if this boulder doesn't kill us, I've got to get up in that tree. Within seconds the boulder's black mass confronted them. Stitch came down on it headfirst, despite the effort the pony had been making to swim to the right to avoid it all together.

Stitch pounded against the base of the pinned tree, only feet from the first smaller branches that might have cushioned the impact, in a collision like a freight car slamming against a train engine. It killed the pony on impact, and the force of the water plastered Stitch's body against the mass, her head and neck stretched upwards at a grotesque angle.

Had Lisl been on Stitch's back or holding on to the mane, she would have died instantly as well. Instead, she landed against the pony's plump, pliant rib cage.

The breath knocked out of her, Lisl lost her hold on Stitch's tail. An endless wall of debris pummeled her from behind, rolling her underwater and forward around the end of the boulder. Her head emerged from the water into a forest of branches.

They tore at her clothing and swatted her in the face. Bark shredded the skin on her hands as she tried and failed to get a grip on a branch. At one point she thought she had managed to get a hold, but the flimsy twig broke off. The speed of the current moving downstream was so great that only the density of the upper portion of the tree gave her any chance at all of catching a branch before she cleared past the sycamore.

Desperate now, she turned her head as far as she could to either side. Just to her left and slightly ahead of her she spied a substantial branch. The portion that came out from the trunk of the tree was submerged, but the rest of it rose out of the water like a gnarled lifeline.

She would have just one chance at this, she thought, raising her left arm to hook onto the spot where the branch poked out of the flooding waters. Her reach missed the main branch, but in her flailing she managed to grab with both hands the first lesser branch that came off of it.

To her amazement, it held against the raging current. Stunned, she squeezed the branch with newfound energy and gasped for air in the torrent that still buffeted her body.

She hung there, abeyant, her body stretched out downstream from her; she was too tired to make any other effort. When she stopped moving, the pain in her thigh reasserted itself. Lisl realized that merely holding on was sapping her of the strength she needed to pull her body onto the branch as the water fought against her.

Painfully she reached out with torn, bloody hands, grabbing the branch closer to where it joined the larger one, and then pulling herself up to the sideways tree trunk. This effort drained her, and for the first time she began to doubt whether she could get herself above the water.

The longer I stay in the water, she thought, the less likely I'll make it. Her right foot found a lower branch under water, but her left leg refused to lift up. When she used one hand to lift it onto the same branch, pain shot from her knee up into her hip.

"Jesus," she said aloud. "I've broken my femur." This made her feel her vulnerability even more. The adrenaline that had helped her earlier was spent. She felt acutely alone, and she was losing hope that she could come out of this experience alive.

If you don't think you'll make it, then you won't, she thought to herself, unconsciously acting as her own coach and cheerleader just as she would have done if she were helping someone else. In the few minutes that she had been poised there, the water had risen several inches, from her waist to the lower part of her rib cage.

"Go for it, NOW," she said, as determination welled up in her to make it onto the trunk. Before thinking about it too long, she launched her upper body upward out of the water. She used all the remaining arm strength she possessed to drape her body over the trunk, like a baby being burped over its mother's knee.

Despite the fact that she had consciously not tried to use her left leg to help in this effort, the pain from it was unlike any other Lisl had ever felt. It was so intense that sweat broke out on her face and neck, despite the chill of the night air. She lay there inert, finally out of the water, but sodden, deathly tired, and in pain, gasping for air.

🐎 🐎 🐎

Elsie managed to release Challenger from his hobble. As he took off she looked where the other horses had just been and realized that their fear of rising water had improved their ability to move around in their two-legged hobbles. In a flash of lightening she could see that Donegal, Sassy and Packer had hobbled themselves out of the danger zone.

She looked the other way, expecting to see the dim forms of Lisl and Stitch coming towards her. Instead there was nothing: just blackness and rain coming down in sheets. The rain hurt her head; it made her shoulders and back feel as if someone was hurling stones at her. She stood still, waiting for a lightning strike.

When it came, it was vertical lightning and ended with a bluish-white trailer of electric current that jumped its way across the ground. Elsie started; it was so close, and the trailer effect so unusual. Still, though, she hadn't seen any sign of Stitch or Lisl.

She turned and fought her way back through the rain to the chapel, holding the oilskin over her nose to breathe. When she opened the door, Lenore, Stanley and Sarah looked at her expectantly, waiting for a report.

"I can't find Lisl and Stitch," she got out, as she grabbed a large box flashlight from an open supply bag and went out, shutting the door behind her.

"Wait, Elsie, I'll come help search," said Stanley, struggling into his rain gear, finding another flashlight and heading out the door behind her.

"Oh, do be careful, Stanley," Lenore shouted from the doorway, over the din of the flood.

Surprised by the force of the rain, Stanley bent over in order to breathe as he caught up with Elsie. She was headed back to where she had last seen Lisl.

When he got to her he yelled, "I'm going to skirt the water on the horses' field and go downstream to look, O.K.?" She nodded her head at him, and he turned in that direction.

Elsie stood a minute on the side of the hill, puzzled by the utterly changed landscape. Then she realized that the spot on which she had been standing, right before turning back to the chapel for a flashlight, was already under water. Looking toward what would have been Lisl's position, her flashlight's beams flickering over what looked like a horror movie, she went stiff with the only possible answer: both Stitch and Lisl had been sucked into the current.

She moved off, tripping over debris in the shallower water at the edge of the flood plain in the meadow, righting herself and staggering on. She came to a promontory that was not flooded and where the noise was particularly loud. Grateful not to be slogging through water, she climbed it and edged toward the deafening noise of the creek.

She threw the beam of her flashlight on what was below, sucking in her breath when she looked down on the rogue waves that were breaking against the small headland that she stood on. The weak beam from the flashlight did little to penetrate the viscous darkness below her.

As she stood there, paralyzed by the noise and the violence of the scene below, the realization crept over her that nothing animal or human could survive in it. Should she follow Stanley downstream to warn him to give up looking, or should she just head for the safety of the chapel and leave Stanley to come to the same conclusion that she had?

Just at that instant, as she was peering upstream wondering if she were imagining a dark mass that seemed to lie astride the swollen water, several bolts of lightening hit in rapid succession. It took Elsie a few seconds to realize, first, that the huge sycamore was down, and, second, that the inert form draped over a large branch—an image now seared into her memory—had to be Lisl.

What should she do about what she had seen? The psychic weight of this question, and the way that it had immediately formed in her head, shamed her, and wiped out the kaleidoscope of horrors that had rooted there in the last few minutes. That it had even occurred to her disgusted Elsie, but she recognized in herself the urge to punish Lisl—or was it Sam, or both?

As she stood there, immobilized by her conflicting emotions and the realization of how much trouble they were all in, she failed to register the first, miniscule tremor of the earth beneath her. Softly, stealthily, the ground moved, and even as she was taking a step backward, she and the eroded bank she stood on eased, with a certain inevitability, into the maw of the flood.

Stanley had given the flooded creek a wide berth; he was in the forest below Holy Hollow struggling to make his way downhill, hoping his flashlight would reveal something besides the rocks and tangled undergrowth that threatened to ensnare him. After a half-hour of this, the thought crossed his mind that he needed to reserve enough strength to get himself back up to the chapel.

As he stopped, the same thought came to him that had come to Elsie: how bad the odds were that anyone would survive in that torrent. Ruefully, he also acknowledged to himself that had Lisl miraculously survived, the odds were even worse that he would find her in the rain and the dark and the noise.

Abruptly he turned and began making his way back up the mountain. Oddly, going uphill was easier, in that if he tripped there wasn't such a long way to fall. At one point his downhill foot slipped backwards, and to keep himself from falling he dropped the flashlight to brace himself with his hands.

The impact of hitting the ground knocked the flashlight off. For a panicky few minutes Stanley, on all fours, patted the saturated ground around him while the rain pelted him and made its way down the back of his neck, up the sleeves of his rain jacket and into his boots.

Stanley had assumed that the flashlight had fallen forward from his hands, but as soon as he began turning his body to search behind him his foot felt it. He swung around and grabbed it, holding his breath as he worked the switch. Miracle of miracles, it worked! He pulled himself up to standing even as the force of the rain seemed determined to press him back down onto his knees.

When he finally broke into the meadow, Stanley felt his heart lift as he made his way around the edge of the flood. At the base of the hill, he looked up and could dimly see the outline of the chapel above him. Something looked peculiar, but it wasn't until he was halfway up that he could make out that part of the roof was gone. The portion that had not broken away stuck up at a jaunty angle, like a skewed ski jump.

Fear struck him with the power of a heart attack, robbing him of the sense that had been building that, if he could just regain the shelter of the chapel, he, Lenore, and Sarah would be safe.

While fear had the upper hand, it seemed to Stanley that there was a disconnect between his mind and his body. His limbs were jellylike, and his hands shook as he made the last part of the climb to the chapel, stepped up onto the porch and shoved the door open.

There was just as much rain on the inside of the door as there was on the outside, but thankfully the section of the roof over what had been the raised chancel had held, for the most part, although there were a few leaks where the altar would have been. Lenore and Sarah were in the chancel area with the food bags and the tack from the porch. It was all in a jumble, wet but safe.

He didn't know who was gladder to see whom; they greeted him with relieved shouts of "Oh Stanley!" He folded both of them in a big bear hug until he realized that he was making them even wetter than they were already.

"Where is Elsie? Did you find Lisl?" Lenore and Sarah burst out simultaneously. "How are the horses?"

"I wish I could answer your questions," Stanley replied, "but I can't. There was no sign of Lisl or Stitch when Elsie and I went out, and we split up looking for them. I went way around the flooded area and down into the forest, but...." His voice trailed off as he shook his head, trying to get control of his speaking voice, which was quavering.

Instinctively Lenore moved close to him, rubbing Stanley across his shoulders to comfort him. He began again.

"You have no idea...it's hell out there. You can't see, you can't hear over the din, you can't breathe right. Lisl could have been lying ten yards away from me and I wouldn't have known it. There is no point in searching until daylight, and until this rain lets up."

"How long do you think it's been since we got here," asked Sarah, "since it began to rain just after that?"

"You two would have a better idea about that than I," answered Stanley. "The time I was outside seems like an eternity."

"I think we got here between eight and nine, probably closer to nine," Lenore said, "and since my watch says it's a little past midnight, it's been raining about three hours."

"When did that part of the roof go?" asked Stanley.

"Not long after you left," Lenore replied. "First the leaks got worse, and then there was a burst of wind, and that section of roof just blew away. Sarah was sitting in the chancel, but she saw what had happened and lickety-split came and helped me move all the stuff."

Reassured to be back and under some cover, Stanley suddenly realized that he was starved.

"Any of that bread pudding left?" he inquired.

"Believe it or not, I think there was some left over," said Lenore, as she began picking up sacks and bedrolls, looking under them for the earth-colored Dutch oven that had held the bread pudding.

"Here it is," Sarah said, holding up a bridle that had been thrown over it.

"Oh thanks," Stanley responded. He found a stray knife, using it to cut away and eat the crusty bits clinging to the edges of the pan. Lenore gave him a loving look, glad beyond words that he had returned unharmed from his search for Lisl.

"If I'm this hungry," commented Stanley, "I hate to think how starved Sam must be. He has to have decided not to try to get to us until tomorrow, otherwise he would be here by now."

All three of them recognized the possibility that they might be the only members of the group that were managing to weather the storm, but no one acknowledged the thought out loud. None of them felt like sleeping, but they were too tired to stand or even to sit upright.

Stanley unwrapped a bedroll, not bothering to check to whom it belonged, and stretched out on it, motioning to Lenore to come lie down next to him. Sarah found another bedroll, and made a pillow out of some empty sacks. An uneasy silence fell over them.

FIFTEEN

LISL DRIFTED IN AND OUT OF CONSCIOUSNESS, aware that she could do nothing else to save herself, and hoping for dawn at the same time that she sensed she had many hours yet to go. Her leg throbbed and her rib cage was stiff and sore from the limb beneath her, but what bothered her most was a searing headache. The pain in her head did not allow for thought.

This was probably a blessing in disguise; had she been able to use her own practical, realistic mind, she might have lost all hope and let herself slip off the tree limb, exchanging pain for the relief of oblivion. As it was, though, she hung on, combatting all the forces that had combined to leave her stranded in a downed tree in the dead of night in drenching rain over a creek that had been transformed into an out-of-control killing machine.

To the extent that she had a plan, it was to hang on until daylight and hope to be rescued when she could be seen. But again, natural forces took over when her limb broke off close to the trunk of the tree, not far from where she lay draped over it.

She had been in a semi-conscious state, but the feel of the cold water enveloping her, and the terrifying realization that she was again a traveler downstream, kicked her survival instincts back on.

The limb was moving parallel with the current, which she could recognize as having lessened some since earlier that night. It was no longer raining, and the waves were not as high. The torrent was retreating, giving up some of the land it had taken over six hours before.

The debris, however, had only increased, as branches, rocks, boulders, dead animals, signposts, and broken fencing rocketed downstream in the waters around her. There was no hope of striking out for either bank; with her injured leg she would quickly have drowned or been killed by blunt force. She lay still over the log, clinging with every fiber of her being in order to maintain her perch.

During the deluge, when the water pressure and the load of debris were at their highest, Lisl had been aware of the occasional loud clap that did not sound like thunder. If the noise came from upstream, it would be followed by a rush of water and debris that challenged her to hold on more tightly as it passed. The noise had come when logjams exploded, hit by something more massive and heavier coming from higher on the mountain and headed downstream.

Now, directly in Lisl's path, was just such a logjam that had not yet been exploded. She couldn't see it or hear it, but it lay ahead, a jumbled mass that formed a blockage from one side to the other, allowing for no passage save underneath.

Her log rode buoyantly high in the water; it had not been waterlogged before breaking off from the trunk of the tree that had carried her at the height of the storm. The log was a long, good-sized limb, shorn of its smaller branches earlier in the storm. She rode it close to its upstream end.

Lisl's log T-boned the jam with an astounding crash, forcing the butt end, with Lisl on it, up into the air. The butt end fell sideways into the rubble, adding to the logjam. Lisl shot through the air, propelled by the force of the collision. In a bizarre coincidence, she landed hard on a newly-rearranged piece of earth formed when the eroded bank that Elsie had been standing on collapsed. Lisl lay face down in the mud left by the receded water; her legs splayed, one arm beneath her as she lay there, still breathing but now unconscious.

🐎 🐎 🐎

Sam came out of the woods at Holy Hollow just as the sun reached its zenith. The day was quiet and calm, as if the events of the evening before had not happened. His walk through the woods had given him too much time to think; his mind had constructed and then reconstructed scene after gruesome scene of what might have befallen the others.

So he was cheered to hear voices as he broke into the sunlight. As he came around the side of the chapel, though, his eyes took in the peeled-back roof at the same time that he saw Sarah, Stanley and Lenore sitting cross-legged in the sun, eating apples.

As he instinctively looked toward the chapel for evidence of Lisl and Elsie, Stanley spotted him. "Sam!" he shouted, and with that the two women and Stanley got quickly to their feet and stood there, awkwardly. When Sam reached them, he dispensed with greetings and said first off, "Where are Lisl and Elsie?"

"We don't know," answered Lenore, looking at him closely and noticing the haunted look in his eyes. "Sit down, you look as if you could use a rest and a meal, and we'll tell you what happened here, at least as far as we know...which isn't far," she finished lamely.

Sarah disappeared into the chapel to find food, while Sam wearily sank to the ground.

"You must be starved," Lenore said, "and thirsty too." She picked up a canteen they had just refilled, dropping a water purification tablet into it. "This will be ready in a few minutes."

Sarah came out carrying a big wedge of cheese, a roll of dry salami, a hunk of bread and a knife.

"Thank you, Sarah," Sam said, looking up at her gratefully. "I forgot to ask Hans and Tad for food when they came to pick up the horses, so right this minute I'd rather have what's in your hand than a pot of gold."

This reminder of the first emergency of the trip triggered questions about Meg and the ride out to the parkway. Sam answered their questions as he wolfed down the food. Sarah made a second trip inside to find more cheese to help fill up Sam. When she returned she dropped down beside them.

"Isn't it amazing," she commented, "that Meg's accident happened just yesterday? It seems an eternity removed from where we are today, and as if it occurred on a different planet."

Suddenly Lenore started. "Where's Rebel Yell?" she quizzed him, as the next series of questions flashed into her mind. "And why are you on foot?" she added, as Sam continued eating.

For the next few minutes, as he stared beyond his questioners at the forest behind them, Sam could hear his own subdued voice telling them the bare facts about what had happened when the mountains he loved so had turned on him.

His listeners strained to hear him, astounded at his story and at the tone in which he told it. There was not even an echo of the Sam they had known for three days; to their surprise, they wished he were showing them at least a trace of the masculine swagger that they associated with him.

The horror of what he was describing registered on the faces of Stanley, Lenore and Sarah. Sam's face showed only a numb acceptance and deep exhaustion. When he finished, no one said anything.

Sam, pulling his thoughts from the painful place they had been, suddenly realized there were no horses about.

"Where are your horses?" he queried. The three that were being questioned looked at each other. Finally Lenore took it upon herself to bring Sam up to date as to what had befallen them during the night. She took care to couch her descriptions in as positive a light as she could, emphasizing that there was so much they didn't know.

Sam's shoulders sagged as he listened. At his core he knew that there could be little chance that either Lisl or Elsie had survived if they had pitted themselves against the power of this storm. He didn't want to betray this realization, however, so he rose to his feet, trying to project an air of purposefulness that he didn't feel.

"Stanley," he said, "you and Lenore take the extra lead shanks that are in the bottom of the tack bag and head into the forest in the direction that the horses would have gone to escape the water. With hobbles on they couldn't have gone but so far. When you find them, take the hobbles off for the walk back. Sarah, why don't you stay here at the chapel and see what you can do about drying out the contents of the packs. I'm going to go downstream to look for Elsie and Lisl. I'll be back as soon as I can."

With that he moved away from their circle, loping stiffly sideways down the steep hill in front of the chapel, the uphill edge of his cowboy boots digging into the soaked hillside. The others mechanically rose from the ground and silently went about doing what Sam had asked them to do.

Sam had tried to hide from them how exhausted he was. Now, as he began his search, he made an effort not to think about how much he would rather have lain down in the calm sunshine, closed his eyes and escaped into the oblivion of sleep. He was terrified of what he might find, even while he was aware of the possibility that he might not find anything.

As he got to the edge of the water and began moving downstream, he tortured himself with the question "What do I want to find?" He tried to banish the thought from his mind, but his mind was as tired as his body, and it refused to be disciplined. He knew it would be an unforgiveable sin to wish his wife dead, so instead he concentrated on a tiny spark of hope that Lisl might be alive.

Still, he was tortured by his own base instincts, the contrast of what he should want with what he did want. He couldn't stand it, but at the same time couldn't escape it. Without knowing what he was doing, he raised his arms above his head, waving them back and forth as if he were trying to summon the attention of a pilot in an airplane above, yelling out loud, "Stop, stop, stop!"

He felt like a man possessed, but when he tried to clear his mind, the demons in his head only laughed at him. As he skirted the creek that was now largely back within its banks, he gave up, and yelled hoarsely into an indifferent sky, "LISL!"

A half-hour later, when he did find her while looking down from the jagged portion of the headland that had not eroded, he was sure she was dead. It was not just the unnatural position of her limbs; there was also a deathly stillness to the body, as if it were already becoming part of the soil underneath it.

The shock of seeing her imprinted in the mud felled him where he stood. He crumpled to the ground, beating his fists on the soaked earth, tears finally finding their way out of the depths of his being. He lay there so thoroughly spent he gave up the idea of getting up. He tried raising his head, found he didn't have the strength to do so, closed his eyes and let the blackness take over.

When he awoke, his eyes opened on a mosquito circling his face. He swatted at it with his hand, wondering why he was lying there. Wasn't there something he had to do? Raising his upper body into a sitting position, he looked at the abyss in front of him. His eyes fell on Lisl's body, bringing memory flooding back. Several hours must have passed, he thought, since where she lay was now covered in shade from a westering sun.

As he rose to his feet, never taking his eyes off the prone form below, his mind did a double take.

"Something is different," he said out loud. Sam stood

there trying to figure out what had changed. When it came to him, he abruptly stood up straight, as if an electric current had run up his spine. Jolted out of the fog of sleep, he realized that when he had first cast eyes on Lisl, one of her arms was underneath her. Now, it was free from where it had been pinned, jutting out from her body at a forty-five degree angle!

"Oh my God," he screamed, "she moved!"

He moved so fast toward her that he half jumped, half fell down the bank to her side, crying out, "Lisl, Lisl!" This did not produce a response, and he began to mistrust his own senses. Had he not remembered correctly because he had been so exhausted?

Sam knelt by her still figure and gently lifted up the hair that was matted to the side of her face. He talked to her as if his very words could coax life back into her, stroking the backs of her arms as he said in a quiet, intense voice, "Lisl, Lisl, show me that you are alive, show me, show me please, I need you."

Slowly, gently, he turned her torso to face upwards. He blanched when he saw her face, which was bruised and pallid, with reddish soil matted on her cheek and a surface gash on her forehead from a twig that was still twisted into her muddied hair. His heart leapt when he could see breath moving her chest and could feel her heartbeat.

From his kneeling position, Sam leaned forward until his face was right above hers. "Lisl, Lisl," he repeated over and over again in a soft but urgent voice, "can you hear me?" As he talked he massaged her arms, as if this might rouse her to consciousness.

Whether in response to his words or his touch he couldn't tell, but as he looked at her, Lisl's eyes opened, stared into his uncomprehendingly, and then shut again. Even as Sam's heart leapt at this brief contact, he could tell that her condition was serious.

Looking Lisl over, Sam immediately noticed her leg, swollen against the cloth of her jeans. Moving slowly, he raised the bad leg a few inches off the ground, until he could unzip her half chaps. Above her knee, where the break obviously was, he would have to cut her jeans to see the extent of it.

Sam reached for his pocketknife, opening it and expertly running it up the outside seam of Lisl's jeans. The ugly, bruised knot seemed to spread even as he released the pressure against it. He recognized immediately that she had broken her femur, and that he needed to get her to medical help fast.

With infinite care he pushed his left hand under her at shoulder level and his right hand under her knees. From his kneeling position he thrust one of his legs out in front of him, and then slowly, painfully rose to his feet with Lisl in his arms. A look of pain shot through her face and then as quickly disappeared. She let out a low moan, but her eyes didn't open.

Sam barely was in condition to carry anyone, even the light load that Lisl normally would have been to him; but his sleep, when he had thought she was dead, had strengthened him just enough for him to carry her back upstream.

She was limp in his arms, and he could do nothing to keep her head from hanging down at an unnatural angle. Sam tried not to think of the distance ahead of him, concentrating simply on putting one foot in front of the other and trying not to jostle her unnecessarily.

SIXTEEN

At Holy Hollow, Sarah had not been alone long before Lenore and Stanley appeared, leading Challenger, Sassy, Packer and Donegal. They had been found stripping leaves off the downed branches of trees just over the rise above the meadow. When the horses looked up and saw Stanley and Lenore approaching, they stopped eating, raised their heads, and followed them with their eyes, unsurprised by their appearance.

Challenger, with no hobble on, snorted as they hooked leadlines onto the halters of the other three, and dared them to try to catch him as he trotted a large circle around them. But when his companions were unhobbled and led away, Challenger, after watching for a minute, fell in line meekly behind them.

When they got back to Holy Hollow, Lenore and Stanley were talking to Sarah about where to tie the horses when their ears began to pulse with the thrum of a distant helicopter's rotor blades.

Instantly they stopped talking, willing the helicopter to come closer. For a minute the thump, thump, thump got weaker, as the craft ducked lower into an adjacent hollow.

Then the noise strengthened again, and suddenly it was in view, flying low. Sarah, Lenore and Stanley waved their arms frantically, scaring the horses but succeeding in catching the attention of the pilot. He turned the helicopter in a slow circle, and they could see him and a teenage boy sitting in the seat next to him, evaluating the clearing for a possible landing place. Challenger, spooked by the commotion and free, galloped away bucking and snorting.

Finally the pilot decided on a landing spot below them, on the flat of the meadow where the floodwaters had receded, and the whirly bird settled onto the muddy ground. Once the pilot turned off the engine, even Challenger calmed down, and Lenore, Stanley and Sarah were able to tie up the horses. Then they waited as the two men climbed out and jumped to the ground.

"Are we glad to see you!" exclaimed Lenore as the two groups met.

"I'm Alvin Stevens with the state police, and this is my spotter, Tim Healey," the pilot responded. Tim, who looked to be high-school age, nodded hello. "We're using local boys to help in the search," Alvin went on. "They know the territory and they've got sharp eyesight. Tim here picked you all out as soon as we cleared the ridgeline."

He shook his head, half-smiling, and said, "It's so good to find some folks it looks like we can help; so far today we've been dealing with the dead."

Stanley stepped forward. "For all we know, two of our party of eight may be dead. The flood carried one young woman away as she was trying to release horses, and the other disappeared while looking for her. We were on a three-day riding trip, and our leader is out looking for them now. What hit us? What caused this disaster?"

Alvin responded, "Hurricane Camille."

"CAMILLE!" yelped Stanley. "Last we heard Camille had made a mess of the Gulf Coast!"

"Yes," answered Alvin, "but after devastating that part of the world, it headed inland, turning north along the spine of the Appalachians, and was downgraded to a tropical storm.

When it was poised just west of Virginia, it was hit by two cold fronts that pushed the mass east. It seems as if all those thousands of tons of water that the storm picked up out of the Gulf stayed with it until it reached Nelson County. Then it just let loose. The whole county is cut off—rescue teams can't get around by ambulance or truck because most all the bridges are down and the roads are shot to hell."

"Matter of fact, there isn't much need for ambulances because, from what we can tell, people either lived or died. And there isn't any rhyme or reason as to how things turned out. Some people would have lived if they had stayed in their house; another family that chose to stay in their house all died because the Rockfish River took the whole house: people, pets, everything."

Alvin paused, as he could see his listeners straining to take in what he was telling them. "From what we can see flying over the county, in some places whole sides of mountains got saturated, let loose, and slid into the valley: trees, cattle, houses, barns and all. No one living has ever seen the kind of rain we had last night.

"Whole communities were wiped out. Flying over the Davis Creek area, there's only two houses still standing. There were twenty-five yesterday morning. Isn't any sign of them, either; they washed downstream, knocked out that new construction making double-lanes on Route 29, and headed for the James River. Another helicopter is working that area—hard to find a place to land, though. What's left in that hollow looks like the devil's playground: great mounds of debris. It will be a long time before this county recovers."

Alvin paused again, looking at the slack faces of the group in front of him and his partner. "But I shouldn't go on like this. It sounds like you all have had a rough time, too. What can I do to help you?"

"I wish we knew what to tell you," said Lenore. "We have to wait until our leader, Sam, gets back from his search.

Meanwhile we will look after the horses and then help him get them back to where we started."

With eerie timing a hoarse shout came from somewhere in the woods from the direction Sam had taken when he left on his search. Five heads snapped in that direction, as Sam, carrying a female figure, staggered from the woods into the clearing.

In two days Sam seemed to have aged twenty years: his confident gait replaced by an exhausted stumble, one side of his head coated in mud, and his unshaven face that of a man who had seen too much.

"Sam!" cried Lenore as she ran towards him, "let us help you."

Sam made no note of her or of the others, with the exception of Alvin. When he reached him, carrying Lisl, Sam spoke to the helicopter pilot, even though his eyes never left Lisl's face.

"You've got to get her to a hospital, fast. I found her unconscious and thought she was dead. I - - -" and then the dam inside him broke and his face crumpled as his voice trailed off. Recalcitrant tears, years in the making, finally surfaced and ran down his face until they dropped onto the pallor of Lisl's arm.

Alvin, afraid that Sam no longer had the strength to hold Lisl, quickly stepped forward and put his arms under her inert body. Sam released her with a painstaking gentleness none of his guest riders had ever seen him exhibit, and stepped back, his suddenly useless arms hanging by his side.

Alvin was a big man, and in his arms Lisl's body looked very small. Her wet clothes clung to her slight frame and her tangled, muddy hair pressed against her head. The eyelids of her closed eyes were bluish, and her normally fair skin had an unearthly pellucid quality, as if drained of blood. There were contusions on her left arm, a bloody scratch on her forehead, and the angry swelling of her leg where Sam had cut away her jeans.

It occurred to Sarah, watching Lenore pick up Lisl's hand to take her pulse, that Lisl might have died as Sam was carrying her out.

After a minute Lenore said, "There's a pulse, but it's weak."

Alvin responded, "I don't have a blood pressure monitor, but she's almost certainly in shock."

With great effort, Sam collected himself enough to continue. "I found her on the bank of the river. I don't know how she got there, or how long she had been there. She has a broken femur, and probably internal injuries as well. Please - - - " he continued, but Alvin was already moving toward the helicopter.

"Tim," Alvin said in an urgent voice, "push that passenger seat forward and use those blankets we're carrying to make a bed I can lay her on." Tim ran ahead to carry out Alvin's orders while Alvin spoke briefly to the riders.

"They are going to use Route 29 to set up a landing strip for small planes and helicopters at Lovingston, but it isn't in place yet. I'm going to take her directly to Lynchburg Hospital. Can you all get yourselves and the horses out of here?"

"Yes," was Sam's automatic response, and then, more desperately, "Please hurry with her."

Sarah and Tim held the doors of the chopper open while Alvin and Stanley gently maneuvered Lisl into the small, awkward-to-reach space behind the seats. In no time Alvin and Tim took their seats and Alvin motioned to the riders to stand back. No further words were exchanged, and the helicopter lifted off, floating sideways in its first rotations like a drunk, but finally settling into a gradual climb to the south.

Sam, meanwhile, remained standing just where he was when Alvin relieved him of Lisl's body, his arms still at his sides. Before anyone could speak, Sam began talking to no one in particular, like an accused man standing in the witness stand.

"I didn't find Elsie," he began, bringing back into the conversation the name no one had dared mention. "I didn't keep looking for her once I found Lisl. She wouldn't have lived if I hadn't brought her back. She still might not live, she has so many injuries." For the first time he turned his head and took in his surroundings, including the three of them looking sympathetic and concerned.

"What happened?" he finished. All three moved closer, following an instinctive urge to comfort this man they had all assumed would never need comfort from anyone else, much less take it.

Lenore put an arm around his shoulders and said, "It was a brutal, senseless act of nature we will never understand. All we can do is help each other." She continued, "You need rest, and a lot of it. The horses are all tied up. While you sleep we'll hand-graze them so they can eat without wandering. When you wake up we'll make a plan."

She didn't dare mention searching for Elsie for fear he would go himself; it was clear to all of them that he wasn't up to it. Sam started to say something, then checked himself and headed back toward the church.

As soon as Sam was out of earshot, Stanley volunteered, "Why don't you two graze the horses and I'll go look for Elsie." Sarah and Lenore nodded their agreement as Stanley headed downstream just as Sam had done hours earlier.

Sarah turned to Lenore, "It's already afternoon," she said, "Stanley has just started out to look for Elsie, and who knows how long Sam is going to sleep. I don't think we're going to get out of here tonight."

Lenore answered, "You're right. We need to save up our strength and go the whole way tomorrow."

Sarah concurred. "We have horses for four people, or five—if by some miracle Elsie is still alive. We can take turns riding and walking."

The same thought occurred to both women as they realized they would be staying put that night. They could graze the horses later, but for now they climbed back up the hill, found the shade of a large maple, and lay down to get some rest themselves.

As Stanley made his way downhill he wondered how far he should go. He didn't hold out much hope that Elsie was still alive, and he himself was stiff and tired. He tried not to think about food or the headache that hunger and tension had brought on. He worked his way methodically downward, following the course of the stream; when the slope was steep he turned his body and his feet sideways to the hill and used his hands to grasp at low-lying branches and shrubs to slow his descent. He went around stacks of timber thrown clear of the water when a logjam burst. They lay akimbo, settled into random piles like pick-up-sticks.

Stopping for a moment to use the hem of his shirt to wipe sweat from his forehead, he picked up the sound of men's voices talking at some distance below him.

"HALLOU," he shouted, his voice reverberating in his own ears.

"HEY THERE," came a voice below him.

After answering "I'M COMING," he moved off in the direction of the voice and soon came to a small clearing.

Stanley could see a man and a young boy, maybe eight or nine years old, sitting on a log on the downhill side of the clearing, eating sandwiches. Involuntarily, he began to salivate. Even before he got to them, he could smell that their sandwiches were made of ham and cheese, one of his favorites. With an effort to stop obsessing about food, he proffered his hand as the two on the log rose to greet him.

The older man stepped forward. "I'm James Shifflett," he said, "and this here's my son, Jimmy." His son looked shaken and pale. Stanley exchanged greetings and then tried to explain in abbreviated form the disasters that had befallen their riding group in the last 24 hours.

Jimmy's eyes widened at Stanley's description of the night before. "The bottom line," he finished, "is that we lost track of two women and one pony. One of the women has been accounted for, badly hurt but alive, and thank God a helicopter spotted us and managed to get her out. Hopefully she's being treated in the Lynchburg hospital right now. The other woman and the pony - - - we just don't know," he trailed off.

At this James Shifflett stiffened, standing very still for a few seconds. "Why don't we sit down," he urged, patting a place on the log next to him as he sat down. When all three of them were seated, he gathered himself and began.

"There's no easy way to tell you this, but the reason we were coming up this mountain searching is that earlier this morning we come across a dead woman. She must'a hit a log-jam that didn't give. Rightly speaking, she was awful banged up. Anyhow, we found her arm sticking out of a mess of dirt and stones, right where the creek comes out of the mountain into our pasture."

"Her raincoat and clothes were shredded, mostly washed clean off her. She still had on one shoe, though. Jimmy and me, we went back to the house and got a sheet from my wife and wrapped her in it. We figured she must'a been camping at Holy Hollow, but wouldn't just one woman be up there alone, so we decided we'd better climb up and see if there were folks up there who needed help."

"Did she have brown hair, kind of shoulder-length hair?" queried Stanley.

James said "yeah," and then paused, looking closely to see how Stanley was taking this, and whether or not to continue.

"That was Elsie," Stanley said. "She is the wife of the outfitter of our horseback riding trip."

"Oh, you must'a been with Sam Crawford; he's all the time taking out riding groups. I've seen him at the Farm Bureau, but I don't recall meeting Elsie; not - - - at least - - - not until today," James said, as he took off his hat in a sign of respect for the dead.

"Boy, did we pick the wrong time to be up in the mountain on horses," commented Stanley.

"Yes, sir," agreed James, "but there wasn't no way you could have known. Everybody got took by surprise. I lost my prize bull, he was in the field nearest the creek, and a neighbor's backhoe I was using is somewhere downstream. I had it parked right in the middle of the pasture where I was fixin' to dig a new septic drain field.

"I guess, though, you'd have to call us lucky. The creek rose 'til it got to our front yard, but it didn't come in the house." James could see that Stanley was doing all right absorbing the news, so he continued. "After we had done the best we could with the dead lady, Jimmy, here, and I started up the mountain, following the creek.

"At one point about an hour after we started, I looked behind me and didn't see Jimmy. I hollered at him, and at first I didn't hear nothing. Then I stood real still and really listened. After a second I could hear sobbing.

"My blood run cold, 'cuz I was sure it was Jimmy and figured he had hurt himself bad. I went lickety-split back down, but didn't see Jimmy on the trail. Then I heard the noise coming from closer to the creek. I cut through the brush, and there was Jimmy, sitting on the ground next to a dead pony. It was pitiful. The pony had broken both front legs and had a turrible blow to the head.

"I did the best I could to comfort Jimmy, but it was an awful sight to behold. Jimmy had left the trail to take a pee, and he spied the pony from the bushes. Wish to God he hadn't seen it—hasn't said much since." James, who had his arm around the boy as he was talking, gave Jimmy a protective squeeze.

Stanley said nothing, but put his hand on the farmer's shoulder, thinking what a nasty shock that would have been for his own young son had he been present. Stanley and James exchanged a look, father to father.

After a minute Stanley said, "Horrible as it is, now the question of what happened to Elsie and Stitch is at least partially answered. If the pony was that badly beaten up, it's a miracle that Lisl still has a hold on life, or did, when we put her in the helicopter."

"I 'spect that'll be hard for you," replied James, "havin' to go back up the mountain with all this bad news." He paused a while, as both men sat looking at the ground, before offering, "You want Jimmy and me to come with you? It'd do this boy here good to help out somebody—it'd take his mind off what he saw."

Tears sprang to Stanley's eyes at the offer. His first inclination was to thank James but refuse, explaining that their plan, sketchy as it was, was to spend the night and then retreat in the morning back the way they had come. But where would that leave them, he thought to himself: Four dazed, hungry, exhausted riders on four equally dazed, hungry and exhausted horses, retracing their footsteps over trails that in places were no longer there, all the way back to Whiskey Ridge.

Riding back to the parkway, as Sam had done to get Meg to the hospital, seemed equally absurd. With telephones out, and for all they knew the parkway blocked, what were they going to do when they got there—stand on the side of the road, hoping a big, empty horse van would pass?

Whereas if he took James up on his offer, they'd have both a guide and an easier way out of the mountains down to his farm. If he had cattle, he would have fences. Hopefully some of them were still standing so the horses could be turned out to graze, maybe by this evening, if they hustled.

Before Stanley had left Holy Hollow to search for Elsie, he had sensed that Sam had been so traumatized by his own experiences that he was no longer capable of leading even as small a group as they had become. It was up to the rest of them, then, to find a way out—and here was James, offering a plausible one.

As if he had been following Stanley's train of thought, James spoke again. "How many you got up there? Jimmy and I can help lead you down to the farm, and you and the horses can put up with us until you can git back to where you started from."

Stanley was overwhelmed by the generosity of this offer, but didn't trust his voice to answer right away. When he recovered, he replied, "That is a mighty fine offer, and it's your bad luck that I'll take you up on it.

"There are three people up there, plus me makes four, and four horses left. Sam is in bad shape from having to get a guest who broke her leg out to the parkway. On his way back to us he got caught in the worst of the storm and saw his horse carried away in a landslide. He was lucky not to have been taken himself."

"Why didn't he get taken, too?" asked James.

"He was on a rock shelf between two swales, taking shelter from the rain for the night," answered Stanley. "Naturally he had tied his horse, so poor Rebel Yell didn't have a chance. The tree he was tied to went, and so did the ground under his feet. Even if he hadn't been tied, he still would have been a goner."

James thought about this for a moment, then suddenly slammed his fist into the palm of his other hand as he rose off the log they had been sitting on.

"THAT"S IT!" he exclaimed. "THAT was the noise she heard. Sissy, that's my wife, kept waking me up. She'd say, 'Listen James, listen. There's thunder now but no lightning, and the thunder isn't a clap—it sounds for a long time.' I could tell it was a turrible storm, but I was tired from splitting wood most of the day and kept falling back asleep. But that's what she was hearing—the earth slides!"

James paused and looked down at Stanley. "We should start on up. How long did it take you to git down to us?"

Stanley found he had been robbed of his sense of time, but he took a guess.

"Seemed like forever, but it was probably only an hour or so," he replied.

"It'll take us double that going up, but our farm is only an hour's hike down, so if we keep moving we should be able to get home by sundown," James said. "By this time in August, you really notice that sun going down earlier and earlier.

SEVENTEEN

THE LITTLE BAND MADE THEIR WAY up to Holy Hollow, sweating in the afternoon heat. Lenore and Sarah had wakened from their nap and were busy packing up the items that had been hauled out to dry in the sun that morning. Sam was still asleep inside when Stanley arrived; Stanley introduced the women to James and Jimmy and explained their plan.

"Whew, are we glad to see you!" exclaimed Lenore, relief written all over her face and Sarah's as well. While the horses were brought up and saddled, Jimmy stuck to his father like a burr, which left Stanley a chance to explain to Sarah and Lenore what had happened to Jimmy. After hearing about the boy's morning, both women instinctively took him under their wing.

"Jimmy," said Lenore, "I expect we'll lead these horses down to your farm. Would you like to ride Stanley's nice quiet horse named Packer, with him leading you, once we get down?" For the first time that afternoon, Jimmy's pinched face relaxed into a big smile as he vigorously nodded his head up and down.

Nobody wanted Stanley to wake Sam, especially with the news that in all probability it was his wife, Elsie, whose body had been found that morning in James's pasture. When nothing else remained to be done in preparation for the hike down to the Shiffletts' farm, Lenore, with hunched shoulders, headed inside.

What a shame, she thought, as she stood over his inert figure; he is in no shape to absorb another shock. Nevertheless she laid her hand on his shoulder and gave it a gentle shake. At first there was no response, but then gradually he began to stir.

Lenore sat down cross-legged on the floor beside him, giving Sam time to come up from that deep place to which he had retreated when reality was too hard to face. At first he took her in with uncomprehending eyes, but soon they shut again.

The second time his eyes opened they were struggling to comprehend; a look of exhausted resignation came over his face. He used his arms to push his upper body stiffly off the floor, and then crossed his legs and sat facing Lenore.

"Sam," Lenore began in a quiet voice, "I wish I had good news for you, but the bad news just keeps coming."

Sam interrupted with three words: "Lisl is dead."

"No, Sam," Lenore said, frowning. "We have no way of knowing how Lisl is doing. But Stanley went looking for Elsie and ran into a farmer and his son who were coming up the mountain exploring the extent of the damage and looking for...others who might need help.

"Earlier this morning they discovered a woman's body," she continued. "We can't be sure, of course, but I'm afraid it's Elsie. They found Lisl's pony, too. The farmer's son, Jimmy, found Stitch dead by the side of the creek, with terrible injuries."

Sam's face was expressionless. He stared at her, struggling to absorb it all. Lenore reached out to touch his knee, as if to offer some human gesture that might give him comfort.

"I'll leave you here for a few minutes," she said. "James and Jimmy Shifflett came back up here with Stanley, and they're going to lead us down to their farm. We haven't finished the packing," she fibbed, "so take as much time as you need."

When he came out of the building ten minutes later, he was not the old Sam, but he had pulled himself together enough to shake hands with James and thank him for his help.

When he saw the riding horses loaded with packs he asked, "Where are Denise and DeNephew?"

"It must be true that mules have more common sense than horses," answered Sarah, "because they disappeared into the woods before the worst of the floods. They must have sensed that things were going very wrong. Maybe they heard the landslides."

A short time later the six of them set off out of the clearing, leading Sassafras, Packer, Challenger and Donegal. The horses weren't used to the big packs, which initially spooked them, but after a while they settled into a steady walk downward.

James didn't realize it when he invited them, but his guests would end up staying three days. Telephone and power lines were down, and every bridge in the county had either been knocked out or damaged. It was a logistical horror trying to get the repair teams to where they were needed.

Ham radio operators were jamming the same frequency, and county leaders were stuck at home because all the devastation had happened at nighttime. To make matters worse, initially they couldn't communicate with each other.

Helicopters in scarce supply were needed to scope out the damage, as well as to ferry the injured to Lynchburg Hospital. Nelson was a thinly populated, isolated county in its own mountainous bowl, and news of the catastrophe it had suffered was slow to get out.

People knew only of what had happened in their own environs, to themselves and to their neighbors. Communities upstream from the county had no emergency services to send to help in Nelson County, as their equipment and personnel were already in use.

The volume of rain had not been as intense, but there was severe flooding to the south and west in the Shenandoah Valley, and even in communities in the Allegheny Highlands, to the west of the valley.

Not for weeks would it become clear that Nelson County had lost a full one-percent of its population. The helicopter pilot flying over the Davis Creek area, a steeply angled ravine that backs into the mountains, knew the number of houses still standing, but it would take many more days before county residents knew that 22 members of just one extended family in that area had died that night.

The serendipity of loss defies the imagination, and tragic ironies visible only in hindsight still loom out of the records. The Raines family of Massie's Mill on the Tye River left their house to try to get to higher ground. The level of the flood rose so quickly and the torrent of debris moved so fast that it swept the family away. The two teenage boys, Warren and Carl, were separated, but both managed to catch, or be caught by, the branches of trees that overhung the river.

In the early morning, cold and sore, the boys found they were within calling distance of each other. By some miracle, they were both rescued later that morning. It was some time before they learned that they had lost both parents, their brother and two sisters. The horrid postscript to that tragedy is that had the family stayed put in the house, as the dog did, curled up on a bed on the second floor, they would have been safe.

Colleen Thompson, on the other hand, made the opposite decision from that of the Raines boys: she stayed inside of her mother-in-law's house. Colleen's family had abandoned a nearby trailer where they stayed when visiting and joined the other family members in the house. The now-empty trailer began to float, but the house seemed sturdy and was a good ways up the hill from Muddy Creek, usually only a small stream. Normally this would have been a safe bet, but by the time the house itself was afloat, it was too late to reconsider. At that point the family was unable to change tactics, although a friend was able to help three of the family members to safety.

When the house she was in exploded with water, Colleen experienced one of the most bizarre episodes of any survivor of Hurricane Camille. Despite not knowing how to swim, she was carried four miles downstream, surviving logjams and mudslides before grabbing the branch of a tree as the current made a sharp turn. It was quite a while before Colleen, worried and in pain in the Lynchburg Hospital, found out that her youngest daughter, Bonnie, as well as her daughter's heroic rescuer, had both died.

The Shiffletts bent over backwards for the strange little group that came down from the mountains and into their family for a few days. Sissy Shifflett took one look out her back window and came right out to greet them quietly, careful not to ask too many questions right then.

Without saying anything, Sissy put the remains of Sunday's dinner on the table in the kitchen: fried chicken, a half-eaten peach pie, and a big pitcher of sweetened ice tea. Their guests didn't get any farther than the kitchen for a half-hour; when they had cleaned up everything she'd put out, they thanked her over and over again until it was clear that their gratitude was embarrassing Sissy.

Afterward she moved all three of her children to a small sewing room to sleep on bedrolls on the floor. One of the children's rooms on the second floor went to Sarah and Lenore, and the other to Stanley and Sam. The drafty old farmhouse took them all in.

The Shifflett's five-year-old twin girls, Louise and Anna, were so young that the enormity of what had just happened around them did not seem to have affected them. The adults and Jimmy were comforted by the twins' chatter as they arranged and rearranged the furniture in their miniature doll house in a corner of the living room, their blond curls bobbing as they built their make-believe world. As far as they were concerned, the prospect of a sleepover with their big brother sounded like fun.

In the doll house, Louise liked having the miniature four-poster bed in the master bedroom on the first floor; Anna was determined that it should go upstairs, "so the children can jump on it."

"No, no," reprimanded Louise, "they can jump on it just as well if it's on the first floor. Four-poster beds HAVE TO go in the master bedroom." Sarah, overhearing their play, wished for an idle moment that she could join them in their play world.

Stanley had made good on Lenore's promise and had given Jimmy a leg up on his horse as soon as they had removed the packs. For a while they just stood there, talking, as Jimmy got used to the feel of being so far up in the air.

When they first took a step, Jimmy lurched forward onto the horse's neck, but Packer, unperturbed, shambled on, mindlessly following Stanley. After a few steps, Jimmy got the hang of absorbing the horse's movement with his hips and gripping with his lower leg. He was totally absorbed in the effort.

Sarah took up where Stanley left off, asking Jimmy if he would show her the hens he was raising. He showed her the chicken hutch he and his father had built, and the elaborate wire sides and top of the chicken yard meant to keep the foxes and weasels out.

In his earnest way Jimmy explained, "The foxes are bad enough, but at least they eat the chickens they steal. The weasels—they're the worst. They'll sneak through a hole in the wire, wring the necks of the chickens, and then just leave them there, lyin' on the ground." He shook his head in disgust at the thought as Sarah recoiled involuntarily from the image.

"Where do you sell your eggs?" asked Sarah.

"At Bartlett's store half-a-mile down the road," Jimmy answered, "and sometimes folks will stop in during the day and buy eggs from Mom." Proudly he picked up an egg carton from the adjoining shed.

At first it looked like a generic gray cardboard carton, but on closer inspection Sarah could see a label Sissy had pasted on that had an impossibly cute picture of Jimmy, with the widest of smiles revealing a few missing teeth, and holding a contented-looking hen in his lap. Under the picture the label read, JIMMY'S FINEST.

Sarah helped Jimmy collect eggs, carrying the basket behind him and marveling at the different colors and sizes of the eggs: some in shades of blue and green, brown ones, too, but no white eggs.

By now, Sarah had succeeded in taking Jimmy's mind off of the dead pony. "What do you want to be, Jimmy, when you grow up?" Sarah asked, as they walked slowly back toward the house.

He stopped momentarily to think before he answered. "Pop says I shouldn't want to be a farmer because there's no money in it. He says I should study hard so I can get a college education and do something else. The more he says that, though, the more I want to be a farmer."

Warming to the subject, he became as garrulous as he had been quiet earlier in the afternoon. "Sure, I'll study hard, because I want to get into Virginia Tech so I can study animal husbandry and orcharding. That way I can come back to this county to live—no place prettier—and there are lots of apple orchards where I can work when I'm a few years older."

Sarah responded, "I'd bet on you, Jimmy. It's good to have a goal in mind, even if things happen that mean the goal changes along the way." She smiled at him as he held the screen door open for her when they reached the house.

In the evening, James took Sam out to the tool shed where he'd put the body of the woman he'd found early that morning. She was wrapped in a white sheet that had been set aside to go around the base of the Christmas tree each year. Silently, and with great respect, he unwrapped enough of the sheet so her face was revealed, not wanting Sam to see her battered body.

Still silent, he looked at Sam to see if it was his wife, expecting grief to be plain on his face. Instead there was a look of horror mixed with...something else. Was it...shame? A guttural, wordless sound escaped from deep within Sam as his hands fluttered to his face. He leaned forward, bent at the middle, holding his head with his hands.

James, who was down on one knee by the corpse, was about to get up and leave Sam alone in the tool shed when Sam moved first. He turned on his heel and left the shed, as if he were escaping a building in flames.

For a fleeting moment, James was moved to wonder how he himself would have reacted to such a scene, and in his mind realized that Sam was still very much a victim of shock. Carefully, slowly, he pulled the sheet back over the corpse's face and followed Sam into the house. Later that evening, Lenore confirmed the obvious privately to James: the corpse was indeed Sam's wife, Elsie.

The first night all the riders except for Stanley slept poorly, despite their exhaustion and the forgotten luxury of sleeping in beds. Sam initially dropped into a deep sleep, but was catapulted into consciousness by a nightmare.

In the nightmare, he was in the tool shed with the corpse, but James was not there, and the corpse was still completely concealed in the sheet. He came up to it, leaned down, and with one swift motion pulled the sheet back to reveal the face.

It was Lisl's face, not Elsie's, that leapt up at him, although the marks of physical violence that had been evident on Elsie's face that afternoon were now on Lisl's. Sam felt a burning revulsion so intense that it woke him with a start. His pulse was racing and he was in a heavy sweat.

Shaking, he used the hem of the sheet to dry his face and neck and then kicked the covers off the bottom of the bed. Lisl's dead, he said to himself, and a paralyzing sense of heaviness took hold of his body. For the rest of the night, just as he would be about to fall asleep, his mind—terrified by the nightmare - would again slip into overdrive. Sleep was impossible.

Stanley, oblivious, slept through all of this, while in the next room Sarah and Lenore, too wired to sleep, talked in whispers until the early hours of the morning.

"Sarah," said Lenore, "NOW I think I get it. That's why Elsie was so sour, and so hard to talk to. And that's why, when I went to tell him that Elsie was dead, he asked about Lisl. Oh, I'm such a dolt not to have thought of it sooner!"

"What do you mean?" queried Sarah, "get what?"

Lenore went on, propping herself up on her elbow and looking at Sarah, not five feet away in the other twin bed. "Sam and Lisl were having an affair, right under Elsie's nose!"

"WHAT!" exclaimed Sarah. "Then why would she have brought Hans from Switzerland to see if he liked it here? Hans didn't come last summer."

"True," Lenore responded, "but I think this affair just started, probably before we left the farm." Lenore sank back onto her pillow, satisfied that she felt she had made sense of odd behavior she had noticed even before they were caught in the storm.

Sarah said, "I'm always the last to catch on to that kind of thing, so you might be right, but then again you might be jumping to conclusions. Elsie may always have been a sour puss, for all we know."

"I don't think so," Lenore replied. "They've been taking riding groups out for years, and no one would want to come if those two were having the kind of permanent standoff we've witnessed.

"I was sent on this ride," continued Lenore firmly, "to write an article about it for my magazine. Between the storm, the deaths it caused, and– if what I think is true–someone could write a book about this. Maybe I will."

"More power to you," Sarah said, as she turned over in bed. "Such dramatic things have been happening to us that I can understand how your imagination got on a roll." She found a cozy position on her side, and tried unsuccessfully to curb her own racing mind.

Thursday morning Sam and Stanley helped James repair his fencing, while the women worked to clear debris and to make decent meals from dwindling supplies in the storage closet. Thank goodness Sissy had an enormous supply of corn meal, so the women produced cornbread, batter bread, and hush puppies to take the edge off of everyone's appetite.

On Friday it was rumored in their neighborhood that it would probably be possible to make their way back to Whiskey Ridge Farm. It would mean fording rivers so as not to have to cross any damaged bridges, and making their way around closed sections of road, but it was worth a try. So on Friday morning Sam determined that they would give it a go the next day.

Friday afternoon, Sam felt strong enough to venture back up the mountain looking for Denise and DeNephew. Sam could make a piercing whistle with his fingers in his mouth, and he had always used this signal to call the mules. He had a different, loud "COM OOONN" that he used to call the horses.

He had assumed that the mules had stayed in the general vicinity and were not trying to find their way home. But after an hour or so climbing upwards, halting every few minutes to let out his whistle, he was beginning to doubt his theory.

Then suddenly he heard a noise that sounded like large animals in the underbrush. Not knowing whether it was the mules coming toward him or a bear trying to get away from a human trespassing in the woods, he stood stock still, looking in the direction of the noise.

Sam let out a long breath when he made out two sets of floppy ears above the underbrush; eventually Denise and De-Nephew gained the trail he was on. He had carrots to reward them while he quickly attached the lead lines he had carried around his waist.

Leading the two mules down the narrow path was awkward but uneventful. When they reunited with the horses, there was the usual snorting and sniffing, ears pinned back and teeth bared, before they all lost interest in each other and began to graze again.

James and Sam had initially worried about Elsie's rapidly decomposing body, and had talked together about whether they should build a rudimentary coffin and bury her in the back of the Shiffletts' property, where the pasture met the trees of the mountain that had killed her.

Sam knew that she would have preferred to be buried in the small family graveyard at Whiskey Ridge, not always perfectly kept up, but at least surrounded by a wrought iron fence that kept the cows out. He also knew that she had earned that. However, the odor beginning to come from the shed would only get worse if they didn't find some way to get the body to a morgue.

The Mennonites have a tradition of helping others in times of crisis, and had sent teams of workers from their disaster preparedness arm into the county with search tools, protective clothing, masks and body bags. They worked tirelessly, took on the worst of assignments, and remained working in Nelson County long after other volunteers had gone home, helping families rebuild their homes.

On Thursday they appeared at the door of the farmhouse and offered their help. When told about Elsie, they put her corpse in a body bag and promised to alert the authorities in Lovingston, who were sending helicopters to pick up bodies. At the same time, Sam sent a message to Tad and Hans that would travel via the family-to-family connection between Lovingston and the upper Rockfish Valley. Not mentioning Elsie or Lisl, he signaled only where they were and how they were going to try to get home.

Sure enough, in late afternoon a helicopter swung low down into the valley and landed in the field closest to the house. It already had two body bags aboard; Elsie's body was unceremoniously added in, and with very little said on both sides, the helicopter was on its way again.

Friday afternoon, while Sam tracked down the mules, the women sat companionably in bright pink plastic chairs connected to their base by a flexible rod that had spring in it so that you could rock yourself with your feet. As the women sat and sewed under the partial shade of delicate pink mimosa blooms, they made as tranquil a sight as it is possible to imagine.

Sarah, as she rocked, thought to herself how peaceful the scene was, and how hard it was to imagine what they had been doing only a few short days ago. It was immensely comforting to her to have her full attention on helping Sissy with her darning, and Sarah began to realize that in time—probably in years, not months—what had happened to them would have less and less power to dominate her thoughts. For the first time in days she felt nearly normal.

Sissy was busy turning the collar on one of her husband's shirts, a labor of love that doubled the life of the shirt, as collars wore out more quickly than the rest of shirts. Lenore, who had been taught by her grandmother how to darn socks, had shown Sarah how to turn the sock inside-out, hold it with the darning egg inserted under the hole, and work the simple crisscross pattern that gradually fills it in.

Their handwork acted as a tranquilizer, and Sissy, looking at them out of the corner of her eye, was pleased to see how relaxed they both had become.

Lenore, looking up from her work, said, "Sissy, you'll never know how much your kindness has meant to us. It has been the great equalizer. Yes, terrible things can and do happen, but on the other hand they are balanced by all the consideration you've shown us. Nobody made you and James do it, it came straight from your heart, and it helps make up for the blind cruelty of nature when it goes on a rampage."

Her eyes filled with tears as she ended with "Thank you."

Sissy flushed at the compliment and bowed her head to her work, but responded, "I'm glad the Lord led you here."

On Saturday morning the survivors, as they had begun to call themselves, each found a way to tell the whole family how much they appreciated all that had been extended to them. It was an emotional moment as the group stood on the porch awkwardly shaking hands.

The women embarrassed Sissy by hugging her, and as they walked down the steps, Sissy searched for a Kleenex in the pocket of the apron she wore from sunup to sundown. Sarah had a chance to wish Jimmy a special goodbye, saying, "I'll be coming back to Nelson County in ten years are so, and I will be looking for you in the orchards!"

"I'd give you some eggs," responded Jimmy, "but you wouldn't be able to carry them."

"Thanks for the offer," smiled Sarah.

Soon the much-reduced band of horses and riders appeared as far-away specks to the Shiffletts, standing on their porch and watching them thread their way, sometimes on the verge of the road, sometimes in the pastures along the road. Jimmy and James were the last to leave the porch.

As they headed for the screen door, Jimmy said to his father's back, "She was as good as her word 'cuz I got my ride, and I'd sure like to have a pony." James paused, waiting for his son to catch up.

He put his arm around the boy's shoulders as he said, "It'll be a while, Jimmy. But maybe you can help me put this place back together again, and earn the money to feed the pony." "OH WOW!" was all Jimmy said as they went into the house together.

It was easier for the riders to get home than they had expected. For one thing, the mountain route had been picked for its beauty, not for speed, and the direct road up the valley was a straight shot.

What they saw along the way, however, was an exhibit of how powerless humans are in the face of nature. It was as if a bad child had randomly rearranged a play landscape: here, a house turned on its side; there, an outhouse precarious in its perch twenty feet above the ground in the branches of a beech tree. Certain spots reeked of the unfamiliar, heavy scent of earth upturned after many millions of years.

They ran into only one real problem, a steep hillside where two cars had run into each other in a mudslide. On either side of the road, barbed-wire fencing that had given way in the mudslide was tangled in piles that blocked access to the pastures.

Silently, Sam, who was leading Denise and DeNephew, handed their leadlines to Lenore and Stanley and got out his wire cutter. It took him a while, but he cut them a narrow path through.

As they rode they passed work crews from the telephone and electric companies. The creeks they had to cross were back in their banks, but the erosion of those banks—and the extent of the damage they had done to the bridges over them—was difficult to completely take in. Even the Rockfish River looked innocent again, but the fields on either side of it, denuded of their rich alluvial soil, would not be useful for farming for many years.

In another hour they were on the county road that took them toward Whiskey Ridge. The horses knew then that they were headed home, and the pace of their walk picked up.

In the past, Sam had always cursed the length of the driveway at Whiskey Ridge; stopping erosion on the steep slope took a lot of work and gravel, and its upkeep was expensive. But after Camille, he would never complain again; the elevation of the house and barn from the creek in the bottomland was what saved his farm. The bottomland was still full of standing water and d. Downed trees now littered the landscape.

As they rounded the curve in the driveway on the way to the barn, they came upon Tad and Hans, clearing rain drains in the road. Hans immediately noticed Lisl's absence, and running down to meet them, he stopped just short of Sam.

"Lisl is where?" he demanded, urgency and fear mingled on his face.

"I wish I could tell you for sure," Sam replied. "She got caught in the flood and was badly injured. Thank God a helicopter was able to land and take her off to Lynchburg Hospital. Last we saw, she had a broken leg and was unconscious, but alive."

Hans doubled over, crying out, "NO, NO." After a few seconds he said to the ground in front of him, "Never should we come." Everyone present knew what he meant.

Tad had the presence to realize Elsie was also missing. "Elsie?" he asked, hesitatingly.

He winced as Sam said, "All we know is that she went to rescue Lisl and died trying." Hans was already running up the road. "Where are you going?" yelled Sam.

"I'm get bag and go Lynchburg," he shouted back.

"You'll have a much better chance of making it tomorrow. I'll go with you then," Sam told him.

This stopped Hans in his tracks. He was silent for a minute, before nodding, "O.K."

Tad filled them in on Meg and Will. When Tad had delivered them to Waynesboro Hospital there had been no wait in the Emergency Room. The nurses and doctors hussled Meg into a cubicle and immediately unwrapped her leg.

After x-rays and consultation they decided to take Meg by ambulance to the University of Virginia Hospital with its regional trauma center. Meg's compound fracture would require complicated orthopedic surgery. However, at Waynesboro they were able to start intravenous antibiotics, which calmed Will's terror that infection would make a bad situation worse.

The operation had gone well. Meg was still in the hospital regaining her strength and Will was staying with a cousin who lived in Charlottesville. Will hoped that the roads would be clear enough for him to be able to come pick up their car at Whiskey Ridge Farm the following week.

Later that evening, after the horses had been fed and turned out, the worn-out riders stumbled around in the kitchen, feeling acutely the absence of Elsie and Lisl. They foraged in the cupboard and the refrigerator; Sarah found some slightly suspect hamburger in the fridge, and Lenore came across a huge can of baked beans, which held them 'til morning.

FINIS

Lɪsʟ ʟᴀʏ ᴏɴ ʜᴇʀ ʙᴀᴄᴋ ɪɴ ᴛʜᴇ ʜᴏsᴘɪᴛᴀʟ bed, her eyes just able to make out the neon EXIT sign opposite her that shone over the door of the ward she was in. As long as she didn't move, she was reasonably comfortable. In addition to her cuts and bruises, she had come in with a punctured lung, which the doctors had to stabilize before they could operate on her femur.

In the blur of her arrival at the Emergency Room Unit of Lynchburg Hospital, she could remember what seemed like countless heads peering down at her, and terse, cryptic fragments of conversation floating over her head, like the clouds full of words in a cartoon. Despite the morphine she had been given, she tried to move away from the pain in her side as they hurriedly inserted a tube into her lung through the chest wall.

She attempted to ask about her leg, but wasn't even sure that the words left her mouth. Something large was in her mouth and down her throat. She felt a moment of panic and claustrophobia when she realized a ventilator tube had been inserted to help her breathe.

But the effort of trying to figure out what they were doing was too much. At this stage, it seemed they were focusing on her strictly as a casualty, and this gave her a strange feeling of detachment. She had done her part—she had managed to survive until she got to a hospital—and now they had taken over. She shut her eyes, but when she did she had the visceral sensation of dark, turbulent water rising around her, and she quickly reopened them.

Then she lost track of time. The next thing she became aware of was passing a series of framed photographs of beautiful landscapes as her gurney was rattling down a long corridor. If Lisl turned her head slightly and directed her gaze below the photographs, she could see figures lying and sitting on gurneys all along the corridor.

Next came a room where everyone was masked. She knew it was an operating room, but she wasn't frightened. Again, the sensation of looking down from above took hold, as if she were witnessing what was going on from somewhere outside her body. She closed her eyes, and this time oblivion cancelled out the dark, rising water.

When she regained consciousness a nurse was spooning ice chips into her mouth and gently asking her what day of the week it was. Lisl had no idea, but seeing it was dark outside the window she replied, "Night time," which seemed to her to be the product of a great effort at deductive reasoning. It satisfied the nurse for the moment, as she smiled and patted Lisl on the hand, left the call bell by her side, and told her to ring if she needed something.

This state of affairs went on for several cycles of light and dark, through which she slept most of the time. She was hooked up to a catheter, a drainage tube for her lung, and intravenous antibiotics. When awake, she was aware of a painful sinus headache, the result of infection from the amount of dirty water that she had ingested through her nose and mouth.

She was roused at some point by a sharp pain in her throat. She opened her eyes and saw the last of the tube being pulled out. Startled, she instinctively tried to raise her upper body, but unseen hands instantly pressed down on her shoulders to counter this move. She heard voices telling her to lie still, and she drifted back where the drugs allowed her to go.

Some time later she heard men's voices whispering above her in the dim light of early morning. After a third hearing, she recognized the sounds enough to rally and say, "Good morning." This time she could hear her own voice, but was shocked by how feeble it sounded. She cleared her throat, which was still sore and scratchy from the tube, and tried again to speak out a greeting.

"Oh," exclaimed an older doctor, clearly the leader of the group gathered around her bed, "our fair foreigner is talking this morning! I'm Dr. Wellington, and you're in Lynchburg Hospital. You were in terrible shape when you came in; can you tell us what happened to you, exactly?"

"If I did, you wouldn't believe me," she responded, almost in a whisper, a wan smile on her face.

"Try me," he said, sitting down on the side of her bed, his feet braced on the floor to keep him from sliding off. "You wouldn't believe the stories I've been hearing–few of them, though, from people as badly injured as you."

But then, changing his mind, he said, "I don't want you to try to describe it all to me now; you're too weak. We want you to rest and heal. You had a nasty fracture of your femur. Dr. Blackburn here," he waved his hand at a young surgeon at the foot of the bed, "put Humpty Dumpty together again, very skillfully, too, if I do say so myself.

"Given the lapse of time between when you broke your leg, when it was operated on, and where you had been, we had to assume that infection had set in. So you're still getting antibiotics intravenously, and we are going to request the pleasure of your company for another week or more. In a few days we plan to start you on some physical therapy, so that when you do get out of here you'll be able to manage."

He paused and pointed at a young woman about Lisl's age. "I've assigned Dr. Hobson to follow your case closely. She'll be back later today to talk to you, and she'll be able to

answer your questions as they come up. In your case, time
will be the great healer. Give it a chance," he concluded, smiling at her encouragingly as he rose to leave.

Dr. Hobson gave her a little wave, and mouthed, "I'll be
back soon," as she followed in Dr. Wellington's wake.

In the next few days, Lisl had plenty of time to try to
recreate in her mind the events of the past week. Lisl hadn't
needed her mother much since she was a lot younger; in fact,
she had reveled in her independence. But now she would have
given a lot to have her mother sitting in the chair by her bed.

Lisl shut her eyes and tried unsuccessfully to imagine
her mother there. Instead, she found herself wondering about
Hans and Sam. Where were they? Had Sam died? Did Hans
even know she'd been injured?

This thought disturbed her; she thrashed out with her
arms, unwittingly pulling at the intravenous feed. This both
hurt her and made her angry, and she burst into tears for the
first time since her ordeal began. The doctors had left the
privacy curtain around the bed, for which she was grateful.
She cried and cried: for Stitch, for herself, for all those whose
world had been upended.

As she became stronger, she sensed that her mind had
been shying away from thoughts of the future. Now she began to focus on it, wondering at the curious objectivity of her
thinking, as if it were someone else's future she was consider-
ing. This must be, she figured, a predictable result of trauma.

One morning, in the throes of this objectivity, Lisl met
the reality she had been avoiding: She was electrified by the
recognition that she didn't want to see either Hans or Sam,
not just beside her hospital bed, but ever again. Tears sprang
to her eyes again, this time a reflection of recognizing her
own selfishness.

What had happened to her? How could this much change
have taken place? She could feel no sisterly concern for Hans,
no lust for Sam's body or eagerness to read his needs despite
his faults. Her world, Lisl felt, was as broken in its prospect as

the landscape she had been removed from by the helicopter.

As she lay there, distraught and ashamed, in came Dr. Hobson, whom she now knew as Laura. The two young women had struck up a real friendship, and Lisl was able to tell her much that she hadn't revealed to the other doctors.

Lisl had recounted to her the parts of that horrible night of the floods that she could remember, as well as her relationship with Hans. Laura was intrigued by this, but Lisl had not mentioned Sam, except as the outfitter of the ride they had been on.

"Uh-oh, what's happened?" exclaimed Laura, peeking around the corner of the curtain and seeing Lisl's crestfallen face.

"Nothing and everything," answered Lisl, pulling a tissue from the box on her bedside table and blowing her nose.

Laura put the chart she was carrying on the meal tray, sat down on the edge of the bed, and squeezed her friend's hand, saying, "Tell me what's up."

"I'm a dreadful person, that's what's up," Lisl responded.

"Something you haven't told me?" queried Laura.

"Yes," answered Lisl." "Sam and I were lovers, not last summer but on this visit, right under the nose of his wife, Elsie. We just exploded, I guess. I feel as if she was bound to know. I can't face her—or him. I don't feel anything for him now. I just feel numb."

"Whoa there, back up a minute," exclaimed Laura. "You were impulsive, yes, and perhaps foolish, but you weren't acting alone, and you can't take all the blame on yourself.

"You are going to find that your body will heal faster than your spirit. Few people would have lived after going through what you went through: they just would have given up. You're one tough woman.

"I wish you didn't have to see anyone for a few more days," Laura continued, "but the reason I came in just now is to let you have time to prepare. Hans and Sam are downstairs. I put up a warning flag that you were to see no visitors without my approval.

"I've already told them that you may only have one visitor at a time. Hans is going to come first. Do you want me to stay with you, or can you do this alone?"

Lisl's face went white at this news, and at first she didn't respond.

Laura leaned forward until her face was not far from her friend's. "Lisl," she said urgently, "don't try to work out your future right now. You are in no state to do that. In fact, give yourself at least a year before you make any big decisions. But putting off seeing these two is just going to make things tougher for you. Remember, if you need a place to stay while you recuperate before you go home the YWCA here in town has rooms you can rent that are very reasonable. I know the woman who runs it, and she might let you work a part time desk job once you are mending."

Lisl lifted herself onto her elbows. "Thank you," she began, her voice wavering with gratitude.

As she continued, though, there was more and more determination in her voice. "You needn't stay. I can do it." Laura leaned down to straighten the pillows behind her friend's head, and, after squeezing her hand again, went to summon Hans.

A few minutes later Lisl heard the sound of the elevator door opening and the quick footsteps of Hans hurrying to her bedside. As he entered her curtain-encircled space, shock registered on his face as he saw how battered she was, her limbs and face swollen from rehydrating fluids.

"Oh Lisl," he got out in an anguished voice as he leaned over her, brushing her hair back from her face with his hand. "I not let you go on trip - - - sorry, sorry - - - it is pain? - - - nurse," he finished, pointing to himself.

"It's getting better, finally," she answered. "Please, Hans, pull up a chair, I have so much to tell you."

Hans pulled the heavy chair around so he was facing her, stretching his long legs under the bed and looking at her expectantly.

Lisl looked into Hans's eyes for a long moment, and in that moment she shuddered inwardly as it came to her what she needed to do. Doubt arose as to whether she had the strength to be honest with Hans, followed by the realization that telling the truth was the only way she could reclaim her life.

Lisl was momentarily overwhelmed by how desperately she wanted to reclaim her life—not just to recover from her injuries, but also to shake off foregone conclusions. She had always been the person who made things work for others. Now she needed to make things work for herself, even as she knew how badly she was about to hurt Hans.

"Hans," she began slowly, not averting her gaze, "I'm afraid I'm a different person from the one you knew before this trip.

"Whether that's for good or bad, I don't know, and prob-ably won't know for some time. I just know I've come out of it unable to go on dishonestly.

"When we arrived in the United States I truly thought we would spend our lives together, perhaps in Virginia, if the work was good for both of us. Once we got here, God, or the devil, or fate, made a mockery of my plans. Sam and I fell in love, he was unfaithful to Elsie and I was unfaithful to you. I think you could sense it.

"I am really, really sorry to hurt you, but telling you is the only way that I can start to rebuild my life."

By now Hans had his head in his hands. He spoke through his fingers as he said, "Elsie dead."

Lisl's stomach twisted as if someone had punched her.

"How?" she got out.

"Went for you," responded Hans, his voice heavy and slow. "You...Sam...marry." He said it not as a question but as a statement.

"NO!" exclaimed Lisl, vehemently. Feeling had come back to her; passion directed her words now. "I don't want to marry anybody–not you, not Sam. I don't know who or when or even whether I will marry, but before I do I want to travel, to explore, to work with horses somewhere."

Tears filled her eyes as she saw the sadness in Hans' face. "As it is now," she finished, "I don't know myself. You deserve better, and you'll find better when you go back to Switzerland."

Realizing she needed to release him from the obligation to wait for her recovery and accompany her home, she added, "You must go home as soon as you can. I'm going to stay on here, thanks to a young woman doctor I've met here who can find me a room. I honestly don't know when I will be home." Hans felt as if he had woken from a nightmare and found the dream was true. Mute, he rose from the chair and came around the other side of the bed, looking down at her as if to memorize her face. Lisl reached out and picked up his hand, drawing it to her face and kissing it. For a moment it looked as if Hans was going to speak. Then he changed his mind, and, turning, walked out the door.

Instead of relaxing at his departure, Lisl's muscles tightened as she realized Sam would not be far behind. The strain of facing Hans and the emotion of the encounter had exhausted her, and she could feel that she had sweated through her hospital gown. Her leg pulsed with pain from the tension of the moment; nevertheless she was determined to hold up long enough to tell Sam the truth as well. The wait was longer than she expected.

As soon as he entered the room, Lisl could tell that she wasn't the only person that had been altered by the storm. He carried himself with none of the confidence that had characterized him before their experience in the mountains. His manner was tentative and hesitant.

When he approached the bed, he took off his hat and stuck it on the back of the chair.

"Hello Lisl," he said, his voice raspy. "Hans told me what

you said to him. It's not what I wanted to hear, but I doubt there is anything I can say to change your mind."

Lisl said, "Elsie—how did she die?"

Saying the name made Lisl's ears ring, and its effect on Sam led to a tense silence between them.

"We think she saw that you and Stitch were missing and went downstream to find you. That's all we know. She and Stitch were both found, dead, in separate locations at the foot of the mountain."

Lisl winced.

"We both need to pray for forgiveness. We will take her with us for the rest of our lives."

Sam nodded his head in assent without looking up. She could tell that he hadn't had the time to process all the changes in his life. She, on the other hand, had been lying in bed with nothing else to think about.

He stood before her, looking numb and seeming unable to understand fully what she was saying. She thought about the loneliness in his future: the empty house, the endless chores around the farm and with the horses. She knew she had the power to end that, and knew simultaneously that she would not. "I'm sorry, Sam," was all she could say.

"Not as sorry as I am," he replied, in a low voice. After an unbearably long minute, he turned to leave. Just as he reached the door, he turned back to give her one last look, as if he was verifying that he had actually had that conversation with her. Then he disappeared from her view, into the hallway.

Lisl sank back onto the pillows. Even though every fiber of her being was spent and her leg pain was excruciating, she realized that for the first time in her life she felt free to decide what she would do next.